MW00963853

Sp

by

Ronald Ady Crouch

ISBN: 978-1-77145-225-0

Published by:

Books We Love Ltd.
Chestermere, Alberta
Canada

Copyright 2014 Ronald Ady Crouch
Cover art by Michelle Lee Copyright 2014

This is a work of fiction. Names, characters, places and events in the story are either a product of the author's imagination or have been used fictitiously. Any resemb living or dead is entirely

FIC Crouc

Crouch, R.
Spithandle Lane.

PRICE: $15.99 (3559/he   )

Dedication

To my agent, my best friend, my wife Catherine.

Chapter One

The cottage where the old man lived was not easy to find on Spithandle Lane, a quiet country road off the beaten track in England's rural Sussex. This area would definitely be the quintessential postcard depicting pastoral England; rich green meadows sprinkled with wild flowers, ancient oak and beech trees, their large canopies casting cool, dark shadows. Jersey cows standing in lush green fields, contentedly chewing the cud. Old brick and flint stone farmhouses haphazardly positioned over the landscape as though without design, but nonetheless far more pleasing to the eye than row upon row of boring urban housing developments. This would be the perfect place to spread out a gingham tablecloth under the shade of an oak tree and have a picnic on a lazy summer's afternoon with a bottle of wine and a loved one.

To get to Spithandle Lane when traveling south on Hole Street from the village of Ashington, you have to make a left-hand turn after first passing a beautiful old farmhouse on your left and a redbrick cottage on your right, then on past a row of stately looking brick houses; just past them is the turn-off to Spithandle Lane. The blue and white sign stating, *unsuitable for wide vehicles*, heralds the entrance to the lane.

Spithandle Lane is about five miles long, running somewhat parallel with the main A283 to the south; the main road passes through the quaint villages of Storrington, Washington and Steyning. The two roads are separated by a large swath of farmland for as far as the eye can see. Whereas the A283 runs virtually in a straight line, Spithandle Lane is narrow and full of twists and turns that would challenge any rally driver. At its eastern end it comes out on the B2135 that leads northwards to the village of Ashurst, where the late Sir Lawrence Olivier once lived before his death. Turning south would eventually bring you back onto the A283.

The cottage lies a good half-mile or more behind a huge rambling old limestone farmhouse that forms part of a huge estate owned by the Compton-Smythes, they live in the farmhouse. Their farmhouse, Saxon House, is about halfway along Spithandle Lane on the north side. Access to the cottage is gained by driving through the grandiose black ornamental wrought iron gates of the estate, with gold colored eagles perched like sentinels atop huge brick pillars, then on past the impressive looking farmhouse and onto a deep rutted, winding lane that runs northwards across the fields and out towards the beech wood.

The front door of the cottage with its thick oak planks and large black wrought iron hinges looks eastwards towards mountainous grass covered hills. The cottage is separated from the foot of the nearest hill by a large hay field, enclosed by a barbed wire fence, strung between old cedar posts. A well-worn stile allows access from the lane, over the barbed wire fence and into the hay field. The beech wood is well to the north of the cottage; to the west are more rolling fields, dotted with small copses and hedgerows of mainly hawthorn. The winding lane that leads up the gently sloping hill to the cottage is flanked by trees and bushes on either side, obscuring the cottage from the Compton-Smythe's farmhouse. It lies in its own little world nestled in the countryside like a precious jewel in a beautiful crown.

The original cottage was built over two hundred and fifty years ago. The present building still contains the huge oak beams from the former structure, salvaged from the old sailing ships from a bygone age. Some of the plaster walls have horsehair in them taken from the workhorses of that era. With its thatched roof it makes a picture perfect postcard. The cottage has been lovingly restored by its owners, the Compton-Smythes and well maintained by its present tenant, Harry Davidson. During the spring and summer months its gardens are ablaze with color; daffodils, crocuses, bluebells, primroses, cowslips and snowdrops. Hollyhocks, lupines, delphiniums, forget-me-nots, a variety of roses and a whole host of wild flowers continue to bloom into the fall.

Harry Davidson, now a widower in his seventy-fifth year, lost his wife Catherine eight months ago to a heart attack, leaving a void in Harry's life that he cannot fill. His heart remains broken; he stays alone in the cottage with only his two dogs for company. Unable to cope with the pain of his unbearable grief, thoughts of suicide fill his mind continually. Only in the last few weeks has he stopped drinking himself into oblivion, trying to mask the pain and come to terms with living a new life without his beloved Catherine.

* * *

Harry was in the lounge at the cottage, sitting back in his large plaid armchair, staring at the fire. He picked up a couple of split beech wood logs from the hearth and threw them on the fire, sending up a shower of sparks. Jack and Jill, his two full-grown Rottweilers, looked up approvingly from the worn rug in front of the fireplace and then lowered their huge heads onto their large paws. They too missed Catherine; they had loved her as much as their own master. Throughout the dark days of the past few months they remained faithful companions, never straying far from their master's side. They had witnessed his rage, his tears and his utter despair and watched him emerge as the good person they always knew him to be. Sitting there in front of the fire with his two canine companions, Harry reflected on how he and Catherine had gone for one of their Sunday drives through the countryside in search of somewhere new for a picnic.

Harry was working at the time for the Parks and Gardens in Brighton, he was getting near retirement as was Catherine, she had been a nurse at the Royal Alexandria Hospital for Sick Children on Dyke Road, in the same busy town as her husband. Back then they were living in a small terraced house off Elm Grove on the eastside of town.

It had been a beautiful April spring morning when they left their home in East Sussex in search of pastures new in West Sussex. They had decided to turn off the main road onto the quieter country roads, and more by accident than design, had come upon Spithandle Lane as they made their way towards Ashurst for a pub lunch at the Whippletree. The narrow road twisted and turned through woods on either side of them, carpeted in bluebells for as far as the eye could see. It was a magical place straight out of a child's fairytale. They would not have been surprised to see Little Red Riding Hood walking through the bluebells carrying a wicker basket on her way to see her grandmother, oblivious to the wolf trailing behind her through the trees.

As they drove around a very sharp bend, Harry slowed down his old green Morris 1000 motor car. Rounding the bend he saw up ahead, in the middle of the road a young girl riding a horse that was far too big for her. She was having difficulty controlling the horse, the situation made worse by a speeding car full of teenagers roaring down the road in the opposite direction.

The approaching car made no attempt to slow down for the horse and rider; instead it sped past in a cloud of dust and gravel, almost sideswiping the Morris 1000 as it raced by. Harry cursed aloud and braked hard, skidding to a stop. The horse, terrified by the two cars began rearing and bucking with the terrified child unable to bring the animal under control. Harry jumped out of his car, not even bothering to shut the driver's door and ran to help the child. Before he could get to her, the horse finally bucked her off onto the road, with the little girl still clutching the reins tightly in her balled fists. Harry quickly grabbed the reins as the huge chestnut mare reared up again, lashing out with her front hooves. Having been brought up on a farm as a boy, where his father had been the farm manager, he was well used to dealing with unruly horses, particularly the huge Clydesdales they had used for ploughing the fields.

Catherine rushed out of the car, on the heels of her husband and went straight to the assistance of the child, kneeling down beside her small body. Harry held tightly onto the reins, coaxing the huge horse away from the child and his wife. He spoke calmly to the horse in a soothing voice. The horse's eyes were ablaze with fury and fear as she stared back into the deep brown eyes of the human trying to restrain her. Something passed between horse and man, an understanding, perhaps a realization that Harry was a kind and gentle person with a deep love for horses. Just as quickly as she had begun rearing and kicking, she stopped. Harry gently rubbed his huge leathery hand along her neck, all the time talking quietly to her in a soothing voice. He looked over his shoulder to see Catherine standing with the child cuddled into her, the child was sobbing. As gently as Harry had brought the horse under control, Catherine soothed the crying child.

That chance meeting with the horse and the child had brought them to Rose Cottage. Catherine had asked Harry to plant all manner of roses around the cottage, which he lovingly did for her, nurturing them along with his horticultural expertise. When the Compton-Smythes saw them in bloom one summer, they were only too pleased to have Catherine rename the cottage from Windy Nook to Rose Cottage.

Catherine had driven the child back up the road to the farm where she lived, none the worse for her ordeal apart from a few cuts and grazes and some nasty looking bruises; fortunately she had the good sense to be wearing her riding hat, otherwise the accident might have been a whole lot worse. Meanwhile Harry led the horse back up Spithandle Lane to the farm, speaking softly to the mare and rubbing her gently behind the ears as they walked. On his arrival at the large farmhouse he was met by a most delightful couple that turned out to be the child's grateful parents. They explained that their young daughter Melanie was very headstrong. They had told her that she was not yet ready to ride the mare named Sally just yet, but to stick with Nikki, her Shetland pony. She had wanted to prove her parents wrong and had learned one of life's lessons the hard way.

It turned out that the couple owned the farmhouse and over five hundred acres of farmland; this was managed by a man not unlike Harry's own father. The owner, Oliver Compton-Smythe was a London stockbroker, his wife, Michelle, an artist. The conversation over a cup of Earl Grey tea and shortbread biscuits, drifted to the subject of the Windy Nook. The Compton-Smythes warmed to Harry and Catherine as soon as they met them. Michelle was excited to tell them that the cottage behind the farmhouse would become vacant in another six months and they were looking for good tenants. Out of curiosity and a sense of, *this is meant to be*, Harry and Catherine agreed to be driven up the long lane to see the cottage in Oliver's Range Rover, accompanied by his wife and their little girl, Melanie. Once Harry and Catherine set eyes on the cottage they were both smitten. They were in love with it as soon as they saw it; they hadn't even been inside it yet. They were like a newly married couple standing inside the tiny cottage whispering to each other, holding hands and smiling at one another. Harry hugged Catherine tightly into his chest, turned to the Compton-Smythes and said, "We'll take it." Six months later they were the new tenants of Rose Cottage. They sold their house in Brighton and moved into the cottage, commuting for the next eighteen months until they finally retired together to their piece of Paradise.

* * *

Harry was smiling as he thought about that day. He had reached a point in his grieving where he was now able to do this from time to time, though the tears still came unexpectedly. He was brought back to the present by the sound of the dogs growling. They were now both standing rigidly, hackles up.

"Shush my beauties." Harry turned out the lamp on the small oak table by his right side and shuffled over to the leaded-light window. He parted the thick floral curtains Catherine had made and peered into the darkness. It was pitch black outside, as it always was this late on an autumn evening. There was not a light to be seen anywhere, just the distant flashes of lightning from an approaching storm. The dogs were still growling when Harry opened the front door and let them out. It didn't quite happen like that; Harry opened the door the first few inches, Jack got his nose through the door, barged it open with his muscular body and tore down the lane followed by Jill, both dogs barking ferociously as only two angry fully grown Rottweilers can.

Harry was annoyed and began screaming after them to, "Come back here!" and as any experienced dog handler knows, it is almost impossible to stop a dog in attack mode let alone have them come back to you when they are in full flight. Harry screamed out again, "Get back here, you bloody dogs!" Whenever Jack and Jill heard the words, *bloody dogs* from their master, they knew he was angry. They were well trained and after a few more obscenities he heard the sound of them panting heavily as they came loping back towards the cottage.

"Good dogs, yes you are. Good dogs. You saw something did you?" He said this as he clutched their huge heads in his massive hands and nuzzled them against his legs. Rarely did Harry bother to lock the doors when he turned in for the night. A sense of unease and foreboding told him that tonight he should do just that. He went around the house checking that the doors and windows were locked before going up to bed. The huge dogs obediently and faithfully followed their master upstairs for the night, where they slept on the floor at the foot of the bed, lying in their own bed, draped in Catherine's old pink flannel dressing gown.

Harry kept the bedroom light off as he changed into his blue striped flannel pajamas and as he did so he kept looking out of the bedroom window. Again all he saw was darkness. He sat down on the edge of the bed, his stocky frame making the bed creak as he rolled into the bed and pulled the blankets over him. Finally, he let his bald head rest on the pillow. As had happened so many times before, he heard his wife speak to him. *Harry, I'm not going to kiss you goodnight until you've cleaned your teeth.* Harry smiled again for the second time that day. He climbed back out of bed saying, "All right, Princess," this had been his pet name for her. The two dogs raised their heads; he patted them gently before going into the bathroom to clean his teeth and patted them again on his return. It wasn't long before the rain lashed down upon the cottage, the wind rattled the windows and lightning lit up the night sky. Periodically a burst of thunder would shake the cottage. Harry got up again to gaze out of the bedroom window at the storm; he loved to watch the darkness suddenly illuminated for a split second by the electrical discharges between ground and sky, to watch color return to everything for that brief moment before becoming darkness again. He slept fitfully that night and decided in the morning that he would take a walk back down the lane to see if there were any footprints, or at least find some evidence of what had upset the dogs during the previous evening.

* * *

At a quarter to seven in the morning Harry wearily swung his legs over the side of the bed, slipping his old feet into a pair of dark brown, and very worn, threadbare slippers that Catherine had threatened to throw out ages ago. Because they were yet another pleasant reminder of her, he knew he would never throw them out now. He had literally thrown the alarm clock out of the bedroom window when he'd retired, something he'd promised himself he'd do when that day came. Now, instead of being awoken by that awful clock, he awoke to the sun rising and went to bed when it went down or whenever the hell he felt like it, especially if there was boxing on the television. The symbolic throwing out of the alarm clock had been something he'd wanted to do for years and on the day he'd done it, he had enjoyed the moment immensely. He could not, however, break the lifetime habit of getting up early every morning, apart from the past eight months when, due to the overindulgence of alcohol, he hadn't a clue what time it was, his head hurt so much.

The dogs were soon at his bedside, eager to be let out. He followed them slowly downstairs, upset that his mind was still so alert, but his body was just not the same anymore. He ached every morning he got up and it was not until after he had made a mug of tea that his joints began to move more freely. Lately that wasn't until he'd actually drunk the tea; something he found even more irritating.

The morning ritual began. He let the dogs out then put the kettle on. When it began to whistle, he warmed the pot, spooned in the tea leaves and poured in the boiling water. He then opened the back door where Jack and Jill were waiting and brought them inside. They sat together in the kitchen while their master sat at the kitchen table sipping his tea and staring out of the window.

The kitchen, like the lounge, faced eastwards towards the hill. Harry marveled at the beauty of God's creations, at the picturesque landscape that he had the privilege to be a part of. For the third time in eight months he smiled again. Every Sunday that he and Catherine had lived together in the cottage they had attended the stone church in the village. Since her death he never went again. The Vicar stopped coming to visit having been told one too many times to, *Bugger off!* by a stumbling, angry, heartbroken and drunken Harry. In fact nobody came anymore. Only the owners of the cottage dropped by occasionally, their visits less frequent now. Harry believed they only called to see if he was still alive, he kept that thought to himself. They would let him grieve in peace, hoping that one day he would pull through; meanwhile they would just keep an eye on him. The one die-hard that came through thick and thin to visit Harry regularly was the local village bobby, Constable Alaister McMaster of the Sussex Constabulary. His skin was much thicker than most and he took Harry's drunken abuse in his stride; he had known Harry and Catherine a long time.

Harry and Catherine had no children, much as they had wanted them. *It wasn't in God's plan*, Catherine had said. Harry felt sad about that because they discovered from tests that the fault lay with him. That extra love they would have given to children they gave to each other and to those around them. Melanie adored Catherine, she would regularly visit the cottage to learn the secrets of home baking, knitting, dressmaking and flower arranging. Catherine would tell her all about the recipes that had been handed down to her from her own grandmother and she was happy to pass them on to Melanie. When Melanie returned home she would tell her mother all about the baking sessions and how Catherine had told her that it was okay to tell her mother about the secret recipes, *But nobody else, Melanie. This is just for us three girls to know until you have little girls of your own.* Eventually Melanie had a baby sister and she asked Auntie Catherine, as she called her, if it was all right to pass the secret recipes onto Victoria. Now they were the *Secret Four* as Melanie liked to call themselves.

The other reason Melanie came to the cottage was her love of the two Rottweilers who were as protective of her as they were of their owners. She had known them since they were puppies. Melanie enjoyed the long walk from the big farmhouse where she lived, up the lane to Rose Cottage, accompanied by her black and white border collie, Rex, running by her side.

Sometimes she would go for long walks with Harry, Catherine and the three dogs. He seemed to know the name of every flower, tree, fungi, insect, mammal, reptile, amphibian and bird. He even knew the Latin names of the trees and many of the plants. It wasn't long before she too was able to identify many of them herself and couldn't wait to get home and tell her parents what she had learned from Harry.

Finally the big day came for Melanie to leave home and go to university, where she was going to be studying law, like her father had done. Her younger sister, Victoria, had Uncle Harry and Auntie Catherine all to herself while her big sister was away. The death of their baking and dressmaking partner and confidant devastated the two girls. Since the death of Catherine they couldn't bring themselves to go back to Rose Cottage, much as they loved Uncle Harry. Nobody wanted to be around an angry, brokenhearted old drunk.

* * *

Sitting alone at the kitchen table, Harry had no idea what day it was. He finished his tea and got dressed, put on his hiking boots, warm jacket, woolen mitts, scarf and toque, all hand knitted for him by Catherine in British Army green, Harry's favorite color. The dogs were already by the back door, docked tails wagging. When Harry picked up his stout walking stick, an old beech branch that he had polished up, the dogs were whining with excitement. He walked out into the fresh morning air, a dog on either side of him, guarding their master.

They walked northwards away from the cottage, a cool strong wind still blowing from the northeast. Harry was glad of the wool toque, far warmer than any synthetic material. Finally, it stopped raining, but the dampness in the atmosphere made it all the colder as only an English morning can be at this time of the year. Nonetheless it was a fine morning for a walk before breakfast.

A pair of large black crows were cawing loudly as they struggled to fly against the strong wind, seeming angry that the wind direction would suddenly change and almost cause them to flip over. At a casual glance they could have been a couple of black plastic bags blown across the countryside at the mercy of the wind. The sheep on the far hill were calling noisily to each other, apparently as ticked off by the weather as the two crows were. Harry stopped on his heels and remembered that he had wanted to check the lane for footprints; he turned around and walked back past the cottage and on down the lane towards the farmhouse.

"Get on," he shouted to the dogs and away they bolted down the lane. He watched as they ran and saw them suddenly stop, skidding to a halt. They were sniffing the ground, running back up the lane, noses to the ground and then back down again. Harry knew they wouldn't hear him whistling against the strong wind. He stood still, arms outstretched as though in a crucifix.

Jill looked up first, barked to her partner and the two of them raced back up the lane to their master. "Good dogs! Good dogs you two, come here and have an ear rub."

Harry massaged their ears as they wiggled their powerful bodies against him. Together they walked to the spot where the dogs had been sniffing. Harry looked down at the muddy ground. There were two sets of footprints; the imprints looked like adult male running shoes. Whoever they were they had come to within a hundred yards of the cottage and stopped. Harry bent down and picked up two cigarette butts. They were the same brand; *Players*.

From the footprints and the cigarette butts, it appeared that whoever made the footprints had been standing for a while looking towards the cottage. Harry could feel his temper rising, the evidence he had found gave him a bad feeling. The footprints heading back down the lane had a longer stride than those coming up. It looked like the two strangers had run back down the lane, probably when they heard Jack and Jill going berserk inside the cottage. When the farmhouse came into view the footprints ended only to be replaced by tire marks. From the look of the tread pattern Harry surmised that a small pick-up truck had turned around in the lane, using the grassy edge of the field to make the turn. Whoever it was hadn't wanted to risk being seen in the vehicle and had decided to make the rest of the way towards the cottage on foot.

Hearing the sound of a dog barking, Harry looked up to see Rex, the Border collie, racing up from the farmhouse to join his two pals. The three dogs began playfully chasing each other around in circles. They would all stop abruptly; Rex would lie down in the grass intently watching the two much larger dogs. As if by some invisible signal, only known to dogs all three of them would begin the chase all over again. Harry turned back towards the cottage to resume his morning walk. He was glad to be feeling better about life and living. No matter how low his spirits had fallen, he always got up to walk the dogs, even on those mornings when he was still hung over from his drinking binges, having tried to blot out the pain of losing his *Princess*. He walked off briskly, followed by Rex and his two Rottweilers.

The lane began to rise up a steep incline before curving to the left away from the hillside. Harry and the dogs did not follow the lane, but went straight on, following a narrow, well-worn path into the beech wood. There seemed to be thousands of rooks roosting in the treetops, all cawing loudly, annoyed by the intrusion into their woods. Many were circling over the tops of the trees like a black cloud. The beech trees were huge, stretching their smooth, grey trunks upwards like giant columns. The trail through the woods was thickly carpeted in leaves, a good deal of which had been blown down in the autumn storm the night before. Many were still falling; Harry tried to grab the leaves as they fell. This was a game he played with Melanie and Victoria every autumn. They would eventually succeed in catching a leaf each and while clutching the leaf they would make a silent wish, eyes tightly closed. Victoria would go on and catch as many leaves as she could so she could have as many wishes as she wanted. Her laughter and giggles and the sight of her running through the woods catching leaves made Harry wish she was with him now. He realized then how much he missed their company and was angry with himself for neglecting their needs, their right to grieve for Catherine too. Somehow he would have to reach out to them, because if he didn't, they would never visit Rose Cottage again, even when he himself was dead and gone. It would become an evil place to them both; Harry could not let that happen. One day they would inherit that very cottage, he wanted it to always be a happy place for them, full of fond memories of Catherine and himself and the two dogs.

Harry wanted to catch just one leaf so he could make a wish, a wish to be reunited with Catherine. At the last second the leaves would evade his eager hands, as though they had a mind of their own. He reached out and caught one, overstretched, tripped on a tree root and fell to his hands and knees, still clutching his prize. Jack and Jill raced protectively to his side. They began to circle closely around him, concerned for his safety, licking at his face and nuzzling him. Still on his hands and knees, beech leaf caught between the fingers of his right hand, hiking stick in his left, Harry thought about what a strange spectacle he must have looked. He began to smile, then to laugh and then to cry as he knelt, hands raised in prayer, with the beech leaf pressed tightly between his palms. He prayed to be with his beloved Princess again one day and for God to give him the strength to get through each day until that time; with dignity.

"Amen," he whispered, rising slowly to his feet and putting the leaf into his jacket pocket before resuming his walk through the woods with a feeling of unexpected happiness glowing within him. He felt happier than he had been for a very long time.

About an hour later Harry was back at the cottage. He said goodbye to Rex, who was reluctant to leave. He brought Jack and Jill into the mudroom and cleaned their paws before allowing them into the cottage. He made sure they had fresh water and then prepared their breakfast of premium dog biscuits mixed with some cooked ground beef and gravy. Once they were settled he set about making his own breakfast. The kettle was put back on for more tea, the porridge was prepared in the saucepan with a little brown sugar added once served. He had the table set just like Catherine would have done and not like a bachelor or practicing alcoholic which he had recently become. He even spooned the porridge into a bowl this time, instead of eating out of the saucepan, a bad habit he had adopted since Catherine's death. He was hungry this morning, so eggs and bacon were on the menu with brown toast and thick cut English marmalade washed down with another mug of steaming hot tea.

Harry sat at the kitchen table enjoying his breakfast for the first time in ages; the long walk with the dogs had done him the world of good and had helped to clear his mind. The distant sound of church bells ringing made him sit up, then it dawned on him; today was Sunday.

In a burst of enthusiasm not seen in a long while, he rushed up stairs to put on his Sunday best, a dark suit, tie and his creased white shirt. He then pulled out his dust covered black shoes from the bottom of his bedroom closet. Fortunately under the thick film of dust they were still shiny. Harry struggled to put on his heavy dark navy blue wool coat then plonked his black trilby hat on top of his head at a rakish angle; it was his favorite one with the cock-pheasant feathers in the band. Before hurrying out to the garage he called back to the dogs to look after the house while he was out. In amazing time that would have made any waiting woman proud and Catherine shocked, Harry was bouncing down the laneway in his old and battered army-green Land Rover that had one thing in common with himself; it just refused to die.

Twenty minutes later Harry parked his Land Rover next to an ancient flint wall that ran along the front of St. Mary's Church, Sompting. There were a number of cars already parked outside on the narrow road, tucked tightly in against the verge because the small church car park was already full; you had to get there early to ensure a good parking space. Harry eased himself out of the Land Rover, dusting the tops of his shoes against the backs of his trouser legs, just as he had done sixty-five years ago when he was a schoolboy at *Shoreham Grammar School*, awaiting shoe inspection and possibly a thrashing for dirty shoes. Even Catherine had given up trying to get him to break the habit. He straightened his hat, his tie and then strode purposively towards the church, the muffled sound of *Onward Christian Soldiers* coming from inside, the singing almost drowned out by the enthusiastic playing of the church organ. Harry walked under the small gable entrance between the flint wall and made his way along a flagstone pathway towards the large oak doors of the ancient Saxon church, built over one thousand years ago.

Instead of walking into the church, Harry turned left into the small graveyard and made his way among the headstones. He stood facing the small gravestone that was covered with beautifully carved climbing roses and removed his hat.

Catherine Lee Davidson Beloved Wife of Harry
Wait for me in Heaven my Princess
I am coming soon to join you

It was still a cold and blustery morning. Leaves from nearby sycamore trees blew across the churchyard, swirling around the gravestones, rustling as they collided together as though dancing in tune with the wind. Harry stood for a long time looking down at the earth that contained his wife, just staring and fidgeting with his hat. Then the tears came, slowly at first. His chest began to feel tight and breathing became hard. His legs seemed to buckle beneath him and he began to sink slowly to his knees, he fell forward onto his hands and as he did so he began to sob. His hat bounced across the graveyard, chased by the leaves and came to rest against the flint wall.

He could no longer control the floodgates and unashamedly cried his heart out. He wept uncontrollably, his broad shoulders heaving up and down with each wave of grief and guilt. This was the first time since the funeral that Harry had summoned the courage to come to the graveside and accept that his precious, wonderful *Princess* was buried below the soil onto which his tears now fell.

* * *

At first Harry didn't even notice the firm hand that grasped his right shoulder. He looked up over his shoulder, through eyes glistening with tears he saw the vicar, Angus McCreevy, smiling down at him, Harry's trilby hat clutched in his right hand.

"It is time, Harry. I knew you would come eventually. Catherine is with you, she is here now; she is always with you. Come, come and talk to her through God."

Angus helped the old man up and together they walked towards the church. The whole congregation fell silent, all eyes turned towards the sound of the heavy iron latch lifting on the thick church door. It creaked open and Harry and the vicar entered through the Caen stone doorway. Angus led him forward to a pew at the front of the church. Someone clapped, a self-conscious clap. There was a pause as though this was not the thing to do inside a church. Angus, sensing the awkwardness of the moment began to clap and in no time at all, the entire congregation were clapping enthusiastically, welcoming a lost sheep back to the fold. Angus climbed up into the pulpit to address them all.

"Brothers and sisters, why feel ashamed to clap, to rejoice for one of our beloved brothers, Harry Davidson, here in the House of the Lord. This is a house of joy, not one of sadness, though we are forever presented with sad occasions.

This is a joyous moment and I must confess a little selfishly I might add, a joyous moment for me. I have missed Harry's rich horticultural advice. I am glad to have him back because my vegetable garden was a complete disaster this year." The congregation began to laugh. "No doubt you all know that many of the recent additions to the church gardens have been a gift from Harry and his beloved wife, Catherine, who sadly passed away eight months ago. Last summer the blooms were so beautiful we had traffic jams outside the church as locals and tourists alike, stopped to admire their gift and ultimately God's gift to us all. I would like us all to say a special prayer for Catherine and for Harry. Catherine is now at peace in the Garden of Heaven leaving a broken hearted Harry to stumble through the trials and tribulations here on earth. After our prayers I would like you all to sing Catherine's favorite hymn, *All Things Bright and Beautiful*."

As the congregation began to file out of the church, Angus made sure Harry was by his side to show him how much he was loved by the people. They were as keen to shake Harry's hand and to clap him on the back, as they were the vicar's. Afterwards Harry walked slowly back towards his old Land Rover, glad that he had made the effort to come.

"Harry!" shouted the vicar as Harry was about to climb back in the Land Rover. Harry turned to see Angus walking quickly towards him, carrying a small bunch of yellow roses in his right hand. He held the flowers up to Harry.

"Mrs. Cartwright brought these in this morning to brighten up the church. She told me to give them to you for Catherine instead." Harry stopped dead in his tracks, humbled and embarrassed, lost for words. "No need to say anything. They're not for you anyway. Go give them to Catherine with all our love." Harry looked reluctant to take them. "Go on; don't upset Mrs. Cartwright over there."

Harry turned to see Mrs. Cartwright about to walk back out through the gabled entrance. Their eyes met. She waved and smiled at Harry who in turn, waved and smiled back. Angus watched Harry as he walked over to Catherine's grave, saw him fill the battered metal watering can at the tap by the wall of the graveyard and watched as Harry poured the water into the vase and arranged the small bouquet of roses by his wife's headstone. Harry stood, took off his hat once more, said a short prayer and blew his wife a kiss before leaving. Angus looked up to the Heavens and said, "Thank you, God."

* * *

On his drive home Harry decided to stop at the Village Store and pick up some flowers for Michelle, Victoria's mother. He looked around the store and found a cute little stuffed Rottweiler puppy for Victoria. He already had another bottle of *Harveys Bristol Cream Sherry* at the cottage and would give that to Oliver, Michelle's husband. A beautiful color print of a chestnut mare, identical to Melanie's horse caught his eye. The mare that had bucked her off all those years ago was now hers. In the picture it stood proudly in the middle of a field with a little girl trying to place a halter over its head. It was framed too.

The perfect gift for Melanie when she comes back from university, said Harry quietly to himself.

"Can I help you Harry?"

Harry looked up, clumsily holding the stuffed toy. "Oh, morning Mary. Do you think a little girl of ten would appreciate this?" He held up the toy.

"Oh, I think so Harry. Who's it for?"

"I wanted to get something for little Victoria. We haven't been to see each other since my Catherine died, they were very close you know as was her sister Melanie."

Mary waddled her plump body out from behind the wooden counter and moved towards Harry. She was in her sixties; married with so many grandchildren she'd lost count. She could see that Harry's eyes were glistening with tears that he was fighting to hold back. She gave him a big hug, a big smile and a big heart, because that's the kind of person Mary was.

"It's so good to see you out and about Harry. How have you been keeping?"

"Well, t'tell the truth Mary, this morning was the first time I'd had the courage to go to the grave. The vicar, he was great as were all the people at church this morning. I'm glad to be back to my old self or as near as I can be, if you get my meaning."

Mary could smell the strong odor of whiskey still on Harry's breath; she had seen him pull up in front of the store in the Land Rover and was concerned he might get pulled over by the police. She wasn't so bothered about the local constabulary, but sometimes officers from the Traffic Division made a point of driving through the village, they wouldn't be so sympathetic about Harry's heroism during the Second World War. An arrest for impaired operation of a motor vehicle and the subsequent suspension of his driver's license would be the last straw for Harry.

"Are you sure you're okay to drive Harry?" said Mary, sounding a little embarrassed. "I could drive you home you know, it wouldn't be any trouble."

"I'm fine," said Harry, knowing full well that he wasn't, it hadn't even crossed his mind that he might be over the limit when he left Rose Cottage earlier in the morning.

When Mary told him the price of the gift for Victoria his jaw dropped. "I could have bought the real thing for that price Mary." The two of them burst out laughing. "I'll take the horse print too if I may Mary, and if you wouldn't mind sorting me out a small bouquet of flowers

I'd appreciate it. It's a gift for the girls' mother, Michelle Compton-Smythe."

"Come on down to the back of the shop with me Harry, and I'll see what I can do for you."

"You might want to keep your eyes open Mary, there was some strange goings on outside Rose Cottage late last night. This morning I found two sets of footprints in the mud not more 'an a hundred yards from the cottage. Both men's I would say. They must 'ave had a vehicle too, maybe a small pick-up truck that would be my guess, parked it in the lane they did. Snooping, that's what they were doing. They left in a hurry too. The dogs were going berserk; I reckon they took off when I let the dogs out after 'em. Oh, and I found some cigarette butts on the ground, Players by the look of 'em. Might wanna let Constable McMaster know if you get a couple of ne'er-do-wells in the shop Mary."

"Thanks Harry, I'll do that. You can't be too careful these days can you Harry? Good job you've got them dogs. Now you be careful, any problems with your gifts you bring them back and I'll refund your money or exchange them, whatever suits you."

"Thanks Mary, but I know they'll be just fine. You give my regards to that husband of yours."

"I will Harry. They miss you down at the Whippletree you know. They all ask after you. *Anyone know how Harry's doing?* they say."

"I'll look in on them before long. Thanks Mary."

When Harry turned the Land Rover onto the muddy laneway and headed back towards Rose Cottage the rear wheels began to slip and dig deeper into the mud. He stopped, got out and turned the hubs on the front wheels to engage four-wheel drive. He could not afford to buy the latest model where four-wheel drive could be engaged by the click of a switch from the driver's seat, as was the case with the Compton-Smythe's Land Rovers.

Harry opened the driver's door to climb back in the vehicle and hesitated. Then it registered. The tire marks in the mud ahead of him were not the same tread as the Land Rover. Another vehicle had driven in after Harry had driven out. He went back to take another look at the tread pattern just to be sure.

Crouching down as much as his knees and back would allow him to, he made a closer inspection of the tire tread patterns. It was the same pattern as the vehicle that had been in the night before. He reasoned by his own difficulty in negotiating the laneway that it too was a four-wheel drive vehicle. It became obvious that the vehicle had driven in and by the overlay of tire marks, had driven out again.

The cottage was still out of sight beyond the fields in front of him that stretched out across the landscape like a giant patchwork quilt. He stared in the direction of the cottage, deep in thought, before getting back behind the wheel and driving on again, the four-wheel drive making the journey easier, though he still had to be cautious. Harry knew that, contrary to popular opinion, four-wheel drive still had its limitations; in icy conditions it could be positively lethal.

Harry pulled up in front of the detached garage, a recent addition to Rose Cottage and parked the Land Rover. His hand instinctively felt inside his jacket, he removed his commando knife from its sheath, a *Fairbairn-Sykes Fighting Knife*, the very knife he had used to take the lives of too many good men who just happened by birth to be fighting on the wrong side of the North Sea during World War II. He had been a knife-fighter, he had taught others the skill of knife-fighting; he was still a knife-fighter.

The dogs were barking angrily inside the cottage, definitely not their usual greeting when their master came home. It was obvious something had upset them and no doubt their agitated state had something to do with the mystery vehicle. Harry cautiously unlocked the back door and let them out, they practically bowled him over as they raced around the outside of the cottage searching for something that had recently been there but had since left. Not finding what they were looking for the dogs charged off back down the lane barking ferociously.

Harry was exasperated; he did not like the feeling he had about his mystery guests. He stuck two fingers into his mouth and blew a shrill whistle that could have been heard in the next county. Jack and Jill turned on a sixpence and ran back to their master, as equally perturbed by events if not more so than Harry.

"Good dogs. Very good dogs. What is it now? Show me."

Jack and Jill searched again around the cottage with Harry following on behind them, still holding the knife. In the freshly dug flower bed under the lounge window he found the same set of footprints that he had seen on the laneway. It wasn't difficult to know what these people were after. The house was full of antiques, some collected by Harry and Catherine, the majority handed down by their great-grandparents. He peered through the window as they must have done and could see the early 19th century grandfather clock in the corner of the room, with its unusual kettle shaped base. He saw the French clock on the mantelpiece surrounded by various cloisonné figures and animals. In the corner cabinet was his wife's Jumeau doll, a little dusty, but of great sentimental value to Harry. The cottage was a museum of beautiful artifacts lovingly collected over many, many years.

"Jack. Jill. Come! Good dogs. You've more than earned your keep this morning." Harry looked around him for a long time, listening intently before slipping the commando knife back into its worn leather sheath inside his jacket pocket. He knew he was breaking the law by carrying a concealed weapon, not to mention the length of the blade, seven inches of razor sharp steel.

If the law can't protect decent folk from the thugs, then we'll defend ourselves. It's better to be tried by twelve than carried by six anyway, which was how he rationalized carrying such an offensive weapon. If the police ever seized his knife and sent it away for DNA testing he would have a hard time explaining the gruesome results. He never let Catherine know he carried it, it would have worried her, she would never have understood why he needed to carry such a thing in the first place.

Harry took the two dogs for a short walk, muttering *bastards* under his breath as he thought about his two unwanted visitors, maybe three perhaps if the driver stayed behind the wheel. He thought it more likely there were two. It wasn't like they were doing a bank robbery in broad daylight and needed a quick getaway. Apart from walking the dogs again later, he had no intention of leaving the property. He decided he would drop his gifts off at the farmhouse after a cup of coffee; he would alert Oliver and Michelle to the trespassers and return home. Tomorrow morning he would call the police and see if Constable Alaister McMaster was on duty. He didn't particularly want one of those new constables that didn't seem to know their arse from their elbow coming to the cottage. They seemed to be more interested in chasing tail-lights than they did in catching criminals, a point of discussion that both he and Constable McMaster had shared many times before.

* * *

Constable McMaster had a great deal of respect for Harry that went back many years resulting from an incident that took place late one evening in the bustling seaside town of Brighton. At the time, the *Sussex Police* had not yet been formed. Brighton had its own police department, the *Brighton County Borough Police Force,* conspicuous during the summer months by their white helmets. It wasn't until three years later that the County Police Forces were amalgamated into the *Sussex Police.* Until their chance meeting, neither Harry Davidson nor Alaister McMaster had ever met.

Young twenty-year old McMaster had been on foot patrol that evening in the famous *Brighton Lanes*, a series of narrow cobblestone streets, more like passages flanked by quaint little antique shops, pubs and restaurants, a favorite tourist attraction. He was walking his usual beat, proud that his two-year probation period was officially over and he was now, *out on his own.* He wasn't long enough in the tooth yet for the novelty of admiring his reflection in the shop windows to have worn off. He was tall and stocky and cut a handsome figure in his smart police uniform, the silver buttons down the front of his serge tunic glistening under the glow from the street lamps. He glanced at his reflection once more; keeping an eye out for ne'er-do-wells temporarily forgotten. That is, until he turned the corner and surprised three well-built men trying to force the door open into an antique shop. He had come upon them quite by chance, not even having the opportunity to call for back-up. The three thugs, who were already well acquainted with Her Majesty's Prisons, violently set upon the officer without hesitation.

Harry and Catherine were on their way back from the Theatre Royal on New Road having driven into town to see the stage show, *Oklahoma*. They were regular patrons of the Theatre Royal and would normally begin their evening by having dinner out at their favorite Chinese restaurant, the Orchid, on North Street before walking the short distance to the Theatre. They liked to be downtown fairly early as parking was always a nightmare. After the show they would take a leisurely stroll through the Lanes. They were arm-in-arm when they turned the corner onto Meeting House Lane and came upon Constable McMaster pinned against a wall by two of the ruffians. Blood was streaming down his face and down the faces of his attackers. McMaster had got his licks in before being overpowered. The third man stood in front of the exhausted officer holding a large knife. From where Harry stood it looked as though he was about to thrust the blade deep into the police officer's chest.

"Leave him alone, you bastards!" Harry had shouted.

The man with the knife turned his attention to Harry, "Get lost before you get yourself hurt and we have some fun with your girl."

A small man who is extremely well versed in martial arts is a lethal being. Harry Davidson was a big, muscular man who had been a champion boxer in the army as well as one of their best unarmed combat instructors and despite his advancing age, he had not lost his talent or his appetite for fighting. He would have continued his military career had it not been for his love for Catherine, who greatly disapproved of violence. However, McMaster was in danger and when most men would have backed away, Harry kept walking straight up to the knife-wielding thug.

"Harry!" screamed Catherine.

"It's okay, my Princess," said Harry in his deep gravelly voice. "Go on back to the car and call for an ambulance, these bastards are going to need one. Maybe you should make that a hearse." As he spoke his eyes never left his adversaries. Catherine took off her high heels and ran for her life back through the Lanes, praying she would bump into another police officer or find a phone box that hadn't been vandalized.

The armed man thrust the knife forward with his right arm now extended, had Harry not sidestepped the blade, it would have punctured his chest. Harry moved swiftly and agilely to the side, deflecting the force of the blow with his left arm bent almost at right angles, at the same time his right hand grabbed the man's right wrist in a powerful grip and then Harry swiftly brought up his left knee, violently striking the man's knife arm under the elbow instantly breaking his arm; the knife clattered harmlessly to the ground, the sound drowned out by the man's screams. In one fluid motion Harry's left arm whipped up and struck his attacker across the windpipe using the rock hard side of his left hand in a karate chop. When you cannot breathe, you cannot fight. Instinctively, the man grabbed for his throat. Harry followed through with a vicious right hook, smashing his fist into the man's face, rendering him unconscious and in serious need of immediate medical attention.

The two men, who were now struggling to keep control of Constable McMaster, charged at Harry. As if dancing to a pleasant melody, Harry moved nimbly amongst the two of them, striking savagely as he went, breaking ribs, jaws and knocking out teeth. In less than a minute, three bodies lay broken on the cold cobblestones.

"Better call an ambulance, Officer," was all Harry said in his gruff voice, hardly out of breath.

Harry was glad that Catherine had not been present to witness what had happened, she would have been in a state of shock. She had heard many stories about him from old military friends, but hearing is one thing, seeing is another and he didn't want her to see this side of him, ever. Before reinforcements arrived, Harry melted away to find his girl, leaving the police and ambulance crew to deal with the three severely injured villains.

They drove away in silence. Eventually Harry spoke in a low voice as though someone else might be listening, "This'll likely make the papers Catherine and be the talk of the town for a while, best not mention it to anyone, if you know what I mean."

"Oh, Harry, what did you do? You didn't hurt anyone too badly did you? If you did and the police ever find out it was you, you'll get arrested and go to jail."

"Look, if I hadn't of shown up, that young police officer would likely be dead now. When he tells the detectives what happened they won't be looking very hard for me; I know the Brighton coppers, you don't touch one of their own and get away with it, at least that's how it used to be. As far as I know nothing's changed on that score, you'll see."

"I'm worried, Harry, what about if those thugs come looking for you?"

"Let's put it this way, Catherine, if they come looking for me they won't need an ambulance next time, they'll need an undertaker. You can take that to the bank. Now stop worrying about it. I was born in this town, it's my town and no-one is going to intimidate me. In fact I'm more upset that you're upset. Would you feel any better if I paid them a visit in hospital?" Harry was smiling as he said this and Catherine knew exactly what he meant by that remark.

"No, thank you, dear, I don't think that will be necessary and you're right, if it hadn't been for your intervention that young officer would be dead. I won't say a word to anyone I promise, but I will be listening to all the gossip. Anyway, I'm just glad that you're all right. You are all right aren't you?"

"I couldn't be better, Princess," replied Harry with a huge grin. "And to think I used to be a playground monitor at a primary school," joked Harry. They both started laughing and turned the conversation around to something more pleasant like the wonderful Theatre Royal performance they had just attended.

It didn't take Constable Alaister McMaster long to find out who it was that had saved his life. None of his attackers was going to make a full recovery; the thug with the knife now had a tracheotomy, the other two were still in wheelchairs. The detectives looking into the incident suspected Harry Davidson had been involved. Rather than have him arrested and charged, the officers at Brighton Police Station wanted to congratulate him and personally shake his hand.

It was decided that keeping a low profile was better for all concerned. Alaister made a point of personally thanking Harry over a pint of beer at Harry's local pub, the *Race Horse Inn*. He was still on duty and in uniform when he walked into the public bar and found Harry sitting on a bar stool, nursing a pint of draught Guinness.

"What'll it be, Officer?" asked the portly landlord, not in the least concerned he was serving an on duty police officer. "Two pints of Guinness, please, one for me and one for my friend here."

"I'm not your friend," said Harry gruffly. "But if you're paying I'll be happy to drink your beer."

"Harry Davidson, isn't it? My name's Alaister McMaster." Alaister thrust out his hand. It lingered in the air between the two men awkwardly. The pub was crowded, all eyes turned to the two men and all lively conversation ceased.

"I know who you are." Harry smiled enveloping the officer's hand in his own, surprised at the firm grip of the young police officer.

Alaister took off his helmet and placed it on the bar. "Do you mind if I join you, Harry?"

"It's a free country, Officer. Many good men and women died making it so, though at times you'd bloody wonder." Harry raised his fresh pint. "To the abolition of arseholes!" The two men chinked their glasses.

"To the abolition of arseholes!" agreed Alaister. "And to the preservation of good men like yourself. Thanks, Harry," the last two words almost a whisper.

"Don't mention it, Alaister," smiled Harry.

"You're on duty, Officer, you're not allowed to drink on duty," said an annoying patron to Alaister's right.

"My friend and I are having a quiet beer together," said Harry through clenched teeth. "And if you don't like it then bugger off." The man, far bigger than Harry Davidson began to way up his options. Harry was staring straight back at him. When the man felt the hairs on the back of his neck start to rise, he realized he was about to spend some time in hospital if he pursued this confrontation.

"Ah, I was just joking, no offence mate."

"I'm not your mate and never will be, but your apology is accepted," replied Harry curtly. The man nodded and slunk away to the other end of the bar.

"Now where were we, Alaister, before we were so rudely interrupted?" The laughter and banter inside the bar started up again just as quickly as it had stopped, now that the testosterone levels had settled.

* * *

Many years later, when Constable McMaster was near to retirement he took a village posting to see him through quietly to the end of his service. He'd had a successful career in the Criminal Investigation Branch followed by a secondment to the Regional Crime Squad.

When he discovered Harry and Catherine had retired to Rose Cottage in the same village where he was now, the *new village Bobby*, he went to see them. He cycled his *sit-up and beg* black Sturmey Archer, three-speed Raleigh police issue bicycle, complete with huge leather saddle, black leather saddle bag and twenty-eight inch wheels, all the way to Rose Cottage from the Storrington Police Station. It was more of a police office than an actual police station. When he finally arrived at Rose Cottage, hot and sweaty early one afternoon, Harry and Catherine were overjoyed to see him. He stayed for tea and sandwiches that soon became one beer followed by another, then another. When he eventually departed he was half in the bag, crashing three times into the ditch before reaching the village.

Finally he wobbled his bicycle into the entrance of the small police station, attempted to lean the large bicycle against the wall of the station, misjudged the distance from the wall, only realizing it when the huge black bicycle clanged to the ground. After numerous failed, but highly comical attempts to right the bicycle, Police Constable Alaister McMaster reached clumsily along the wall until he found the door, opened it and fell in, sprawling across the floor. He pulled himself up into a chair in the police office and sat there with a stupid grin on his face.

When his colleagues found him sitting like a drunken sailor in a dockside tavern, snoring and stinking of booze, they quickly tucked him away in the sergeant's office out of the public gaze. Fortunately, Sergeant Harris had just left the office prior to the ungainly arrival of Constable McMaster ringing the bicycle bell as loud as he could all the way through the village. Even though Harris never witnessed the spectacle he got to hear about it and was constantly reminded of it by the public for years afterwards.

Alaister made a point of looking in on Harry and Catherine every couple of weeks, mainly by police car, except in the summer when he liked to keep fit riding the bicycle. He believed the *Brass* let him use it because they thought they were punishing him, he never let them know how much he loved cycling. When Catherine died he was probably the one person that kept Harry going. Whereas everybody else eventually drifted away, Alaister wouldn't. He made sure Harry was eating properly and sometimes helped with the dogs, who eventually grew to trust him. In Alaister's mind, Harry had saved his life and because of that he would never give up on him.

Chapter Two

Making coffee was a ritual for Harry. From the first drop to the last, he found the whole process quite therapeutic. He had spent some time in Canada during his army days on various training exercises. It was there that he discovered percolated coffee. On his return to England he brought a percolator back with him and gave away his remaining jar of ghastly tasting instant coffee. He never touched the stuff again.

The kitchen began to fill with that wonderful aroma of freshly percolated coffee. As the contraption hissed away like some piece of apparatus in a chemistry experiment, Harry poured a little cream into the bottom of his cup and a spoonful of brown sugar. He liked a mug for his tea and a cup for his coffee. He wasn't too bothered about which mug he had for his tea, but the coffee cup had to be the right one. It was a large off-white cup with real gold around the rim and had a picture of two Clydesdale horses pulling a huge cart laden with hay. The matching saucer didn't quite match anymore. Catherine had dropped it when she was washing up. It broke into two pieces in front of Harry. He could see her standing there before him saying, *Oh, Harry, I'm so sorry!* He bent down and picked up the two pieces. *It's only a saucer Princess, nothing a little bit of glue won't fix, now don't you fret.* He had given her a hug to reassure her that he really wasn't that bothered.

Harry now looked down at the saucer and the crack that didn't quite glue together as perfectly as he had planned. Somehow it had shifted slightly in the gluing process making the cup wobble just a little when placed on top of the saucer. He'd have given anything to have Catherine walk back into the kitchen and drop the cup into a thousand pieces on the stone floor so he could hug her again, just one more time. He sighed; this time he didn't cry and began to smile as he thought of that morning. Catherine had gone out that very day and bought him another expensive cup and saucer with a real gold rim and this time a picture of a cottage on the front, not unlike Rose Cottage. He had never used it; instead he proudly displayed it in the corner cabinet in the lounge. He had given her a big hug that afternoon too when she got back from the village with it. *At least you won't feel so bad now when you drop the cup,* he had said, and they both laughed.

Many times Harry had been asked what the secret of his happiness was. He answered in one word, *Catherine.*

* * *

"All right, you dogs, we're off to see the posh folk down the lane. Now mind you watch your manners. We won't be long mind you; I'm not one for visiting folk."

Harry felt so much more at ease once he was out of his *Sunday best* and back into his more rural looking clothes. He grabbed his cloth cap this time, the weather having taken a turn for the better, walked out of the back door with the dogs and then came back in again, having forgotten the bottle of sherry. Together they marched off down the lane to visit the Compton-Smythes.

The two Rottweilers sat like minders on either side of their master as he pulled the wrought iron handle down; this was located in the wall to the right of the huge imposing door that led into the massive hallway of Saxon House. Deep within the mansion, which would more aptly describe the place, came the sound of a bell ringing followed by the muffled sound of Rex barking from somewhere inside the house.

Latches were turned on the inside and the huge door was swung open by Michelle, a tall thin brunette in her mid-forties. A very attractive woman who encouraged healthy eating and plenty of exercise. Harry secretly wondered if he should have brought her a bunch of broccoli instead of flowers. She held the door in one hand and an artist's paintbrush in the other. She had a smudge of burnt umber on her nose that made her look quite cute. Rex barreled out the door to play with Jack and Jill, they wouldn't move until

Harry gave them the okay, and then they were gone too, chasing each other back up the lane.

"Harry, come on in. How are you? We've missed you terribly. Victoria was saying only this morning that she was going up to see you. She has something for you. She talks about you all the time. Please excuse my painting clothes I have another commission I just have to get finished."

"Catherine always loved your watercolor classes, Michelle."

"She was a great student, a natural artist and very gifted."

"I have some of her paintings hanging at home. She didn't really want me to display them; she didn't think they were that good."

"Not that good? I had some of my clients offering good money to buy some of her work. She never sold any because she knew how much you loved her paintings."

"Really?" Harry was genuinely taken aback.

"Yes, really, Harry. I'm surprised you didn't know that." Harry stood just inside the door feeling awkward and not wanting to impose any further.

"These flowers are for you, Michelle. There's a bottle of sherry here for Oliver and I have a picture I'd like you to leave in Melanie's bedroom for when she comes back from university."

"Well, hello, stranger!" Oliver Compton-Smythe strode out of his study. He was a tall, rugged looking man with chiseled features and jet-black hair. He was almost a *pretty boy*, but not quite. He was as much at home splitting logs by axe as he was on the polo field or making his millions in the stock market. The only thing that irritated Harry about Oliver was his aristocratic voice. It made him immediately think of Prince Charles. Other than that he was a fine chap and a good landlord. The two men shook hands firmly.

"For me? Why, thank you Harry, that's very generous of you." Oliver held up the bottle of sherry with obvious pleasure."

"Yes, very generous Harry, the flowers are beautiful; you really are a darling. Are you sure you won't come in?"

"No, that's okay, thanks Michelle. Oh, this is for Victoria. I'm sorry I didn't wrap it."

"Oh, it's so sweet Harry, she'll love it." Michelle turned her head and called down the hallway. "Victoria. You'll never guess who's here!"

Victoria came down the long winding staircase holding something square in her hand. It looked like a framed picture, but the actual picture was tucked tightly against her skinny body.

"I knew you'd come back, Uncle Harry!" She burst into a huge smile and ran down the rest of the stairs in her eagerness to see her Harry, almost tripping over her feet. Harry bent down and Victoria threw her arms around his broad neck. When Harry stood up the tears were silently pouring down his face. He couldn't speak.

"Harry's got something for you," said Michelle, placing a comforting arm around him.

"I've got something for you too, Uncle Harry." She turned the picture around. It was a childlike watercolor painting of Rose Cottage with four people standing together in the sunshine, smiling.

"That's you, that's Melanie, that's me and that's Auntie Catherine. There's Jack and Jill playing with Rex and that's your old Land Rover. Mummy helped me with it and I helped her frame it."

"It's beautiful Victoria, my little fairy. I'm going to hang it up in my bedroom as soon as I get home, so that every night when I go to bed I can look at it and fall asleep with happy thoughts. Thank you so much, Victoria, and Mummy for helping you. I hope you like what I've got for you." He handed Victoria the small stuffed Rottweiler puppy. She squealed with delight, hugging and kissing it.

"Thank you, thank you, Uncle Harry! He's my best present ever. I'm going to sleep with him every night and have happy thoughts." She turned and ran straight back up to her bedroom clutching her puppy tightly.

"Well, I best be off then. Oh, I meant to ask you. You haven't seen a vehicle driving up the lane to Rose Cottage have you? There was one last night and one this morning. Not that I saw it myself, but the tread pattern left behind doesn't match any of the vehicles on this estate. Something was going on outside my cottage late last night; I know that much, the dogs were going mad."

"I haven't seen anything Harry, not unless Jim's had the lads up repairing the fence over in the north field. I told them not to bother with that until the spring," remarked Oliver.

"Come to think of it, I did see a red pick-up truck coming back down the lane this morning, about twenty minutes after I saw you drive out Harry," said Michelle, a concerned look on her face. "It was a newer model, a Ford I think, with two men in it. They looked to be in their early twenties. By the time I went to the window to get the license plate they were gone. Is everything all right?"

"Well, I wasn't too concerned until I saw footprints in the flowerbed outside the lounge window this morning, two sets of 'em."

"I'll tell the lads to keep their eyes open. Have you called the police yet, Harry?"

"No, not yet Oliver. I'll call tomorrow and see if I can get a hold of Alaister McMaster."

"McMaster, yes, good chap. You don't want him on your tail if you're up to no good. Tenacious old bugger that one. Thinks highly of you, Harry, always asks after you when I meet him in the village. Wouldn't want to get on the wrong side of him though, I hear he's a bit of a scrapper."

"Isn't he retiring soon, darling?"

"I do believe he is, summer of next year actually. Well, that's what the chief constable was telling me when I met him at Cowdry Park last time I played polo. Shame they never promoted him, he'd have this police force whipped into shape in no time."

"That, he would. Well, I'll keep you posted and thanks again for keeping an eye on me."

"Not at all Harry, it's wonderful to see you back to your old self."

"Catherine would be proud of you, Harry," added Michelle embracing the old man, hugging him with real affection. "Welcome back Harry, we missed you."

"Yes, we did," added Oliver, genuinely meaning it.

Harry turned and began walking back towards Rose Cottage, clutching Victoria's painting under his arm and feeling a sense of joy warming his heart.

"Come on, you dogs! Get on home. Rex, I'm really going to have to take you in hand you know. You are the most disobedient dog I've ever met, but I love you just the same. Okay, you can play up at the cottage for a while then you must go home."

Harry strolled back up the lane to Rose Cottage. His heart was no longer heavy, in fact he felt quite joyful. He looked up at the sky and smiled, feeling that Catherine was walking beside him. The moment was so real he could smell her perfume. Up ahead the dogs played boisterously together.

"Ah, the times we walked up this lane together, Catherine, arm in arm like a couple of teenagers in love. Thank you, my love, for sharing your life with me, for loving me and for bringing such happiness to my life. Most of all, thank you for bringing me to Rose Cottage when at first I doubted the wisdom of the move. I miss you so much, my Princess."

Harry said all this out loud to the wind, the sky, the trees, and to any animal that cared to listen. This time he didn't shed a tear. He stopped to look across the hay field to his right, soaking in the rural view over the barbed wire fence. He and Catherine always loved the rotation of crops and livestock. Each year the landscape would change, sometimes there would be fields of corn, sometimes winter wheat or oats, sometimes soy beans. One year there were graceful horses occupying the hay field and one year there were cattle. The year before there had been sheep and when the spring lambs arrived Catherine would be glued to the lounge window as though it was a big screen television.

* * *

The first thing Harry did when he got home was to hang Victoria's painting on his bedroom wall. He knew the next time she came for a visit to Rose Cottage, she would run up the stairs and straight into his bedroom to make sure it was positioned so that it was the last thing Harry saw when he closed his eyes. He had always looked forward to her coming and didn't realize until today how much he missed her visits.

"Right then, you dogs, this evening I am taking a brave step. I am getting out the pressure cooker, yes, the pressure cooker. Hopefully, I will remember what Catherine used to do to make the whole thing come together. The good news is; if it is a success, you two will share in its delights. All right then, let's cut that beef up, throw in a few carrots, turnips, lots of parsnips, salt and pepper and tons of garlic, because Catherine always hated garlic and, la pièce de résistance, a bottle of Guinness. Make that two bottles of Guinness, one for the pot and one for the chef, plus mashed potatoes drowning in thick gravy. And, for dessert, another bottle of Guinness."

That Sunday evening Harry sat in front of the television with his dinner tray on his lap indulging himself for the first time in ages, by watching an action movie and having dinner and a beer at the same time. Jack and Jill lay sleeping contentedly in front of the log fire. When

Dancing with Wolves was over, Harry left the two dogs sleeping by the fire and went into the kitchen to clean up.

Catherine hated to come down in the morning to dirty dishes in the sink and always insisted, despite Harry's protestations that they be done that night. Harry felt as though Catherine was right there beside him, the feeling gave him great comfort. Finally, the kitchen cleaned, as Catherine would have liked it, Harry let the dogs out quickly. When they returned they all retired upstairs to bed.

With the two dogs at the end of his bed, Harry began reading his new novel, *Burning Angel* by his favorite author, *James Lee Burke.* He dreaded to think what the fine would be; he hadn't been back to the library since before Catherine's death. The library was a place they both enjoyed going to regularly, particularly as Catherine was an avid reader. By the time Harry had read one novel, she was already engrossed in her third. After they had selected what they wanted to read, they made a point of choosing a story tape together, one they would listen to snuggled up in bed early in the evening. After her death, Harry didn't think he would ever be able to listen to a story tape in bed again, but he was proud that he was back to reading in bed, something he had always enjoyed doing.

Harry addressed the dogs. "Perhaps I'll get a story tape tomorrow and we'll listen to it in the lounge instead. We'll sit together in the evening in front of a roaring fire, with all the lights off and a nice glass of sherry in hand." Jack and Jill raised their heads over the foot of the bed; it looked as though they were smiling at their master. "I know, a *Sherlock Holmes* mystery."

Chapter Three

The weather is a strange thing. One day it can be a howling gale and the next, brilliant sunshine, such was the weather that greeted Harry the following morning. A beam of sunlight poured in through the bedroom window across the room onto Harry's bed. The unseen dust was now visible in the shaft of golden light, sparkling like glitter. It disappeared and reappeared as the dust particles danced between the sunlight and the darker recesses within the bedroom.

Harry opened his eyes. He had slept well and felt refreshed; he felt like his old self again. Jack and Jill sensed a return to normality and nuzzled their snouts against their master, urging him to join them on this beautiful sunny morning. He swept back the bed covers, swung his legs over the bed and rubbed the two dogs roughly on their heads and ears.

"Good morning, my beauties. What a glorious morning. Okay, let's get you outside for a pee and Lord knows I need one too. Right then, big breakfast this morning followed by a long walk. Come on then let's get cracking!"

Harry let the dogs out, got dressed, and let them back in. He ate a hearty breakfast and gave a little extra food to the dogs, as they were going on a long walk together. He grabbed his hiking stick and as an afterthought he slung his binoculars around his neck, tucking them just inside his jacket to stop them bumping up and down on his chest as he walked. When Jack and Jill saw the knapsack coming out they knew they were going on *the long walk*. They were so excited, even their master had an extra spring to his step this morning. They already knew they were not making the loop through the beech wood, which was one of the shorter walks. This hike would take them at least three hours.

It was a long, but pleasant hike to the beech wood. Harry followed the trail through the meadow, across fields and along rough tracks made by the Compton-Smyth's various agricultural vehicles. He followed the familiar track through the beech wood; he had been this way a thousand times or more and could have done it blindfolded. Harry didn't follow the left curve at the end, but walked straight on. Eventually he emerged into sunlight; ahead of him was the most daunting part of the journey, made more and more arduous by his increasing years, a fact that frustrated him enormously.

Harry marched on past wayfaring trees, elderberry trees full of fruit and as he began the steep climb up the mountainous hillside where the soil was more impoverished, he brushed gently against prickly gorse bushes with their bright yellow flowers. Periodically he would have to call back the dogs from chasing after a rabbit or the occasional hare. The path uphill eventually swung around to the right, away from the beech wood, in a long sweeping arc before dropping back down into a steep valley, the track continuing along the valley floor. Harry would turn off, again to his right long before reaching the other end of the valley. He would then begin another grueling climb up hill before descending again on the other side towards Rose Cottage, separated from the foot of the steep slope by the hay field and then across the familiar stile and over the barbed wire fence and back to the comfort of Rose Cottage.

Skylarks flitted around, dropping to the grassland and then rising up again, their singing adding to the rural orchestral sounds cherished by Harry. On a long walk Harry always brought his small knapsack with him containing some lightweight wet weather clothing, a thermos of hot soup and some crackers. The climb to the top of the hill had not been Harry's most favorite part of the journey. The older he got the steeper and harder the climb seemed to get. The view from the top was always worth the climb.

Exhausted, Harry eventually arrived at the top of the hill, it had taken him over two hours to get there since leaving the cottage. His knee joints ached like a bastard, far worse than he could remember. He was thankful he didn't smoke and wondered how many more times he would be able to climb the hill before having to take a less arduous route. He was out of condition and in some discomfort. Standing on top of the hill he caught his breath and held on to his hiking stick for support.

His eyes traced the path along the lane from Rose Cottage that now looked like a doll's house, and all the way to Saxon House by Spithandle Lane, then he followed the road all the way into the village where he glimpsed the church spire way off in the distance. The very church he had been in yesterday where his Catherine was now resting and where he would be resting one day with her. Jack and Jill sat down beside him showing little sign of fatigue.

On the downward slope, just over the ridge Harry stopped at another favorite spot where he liked to rest sometimes, depending on the weather, before descending the remainder of the hill and onward towards Rose Cottage. The sun was still bright, making the hike all the more pleasant. It was a little cool though, being the autumn. A large indentation in the side of the hill afforded shelter from three sides and a clear view towards the west. As of yet, it was still too early in the day for the sun to have crested the hill. Being in shadow it was cooler on this side of the hill, but it was out of the wind and sheltered, compensating for the slight drop in temperature, unless of course the wind shifted position and began blowing from the west. This was the perfect spot to stop for a snack before climbing the rest of the way down.

Sitting in the long grass with his dogs, Harry raised the binoculars to his eyes and scanned the countryside in front of him. He lowered the binoculars and as he did so his eye caught the familiar hover of a kestrel, quickly he raised the binoculars again and trained them on the hawk. Suddenly it dropped like a stone to the ground; Harry was unable to follow its descent with the binoculars. It flew out of the grass again tightly clutching a small animal in its talons; possibly a mouse or a vole he thought.

Harry lent back against the hill and unscrewed the top of his thermos flask and poured himself a cup of hot homemade soup made from last night's stew. He opened the small bag of crackers, sharing most of them with the dogs. All three lay back in the long grass resting against each other, Harry could feel the warmth of their bodies against his sides and cuddled them closer to him, their heads now resting contentedly on his chest. These were the moments when Harry really enjoyed the freedom that retirement had given him; no buses or trains to catch, no deadlines to meet. No need to rush home to get ready for work in the morning. No need to do anything. He could stay here all day if he wanted to. The best part of all; it was free, it didn't cost a penny, all he needed was his health. As he looked out across the beautiful English countryside, Harry said aloud, "You can't put a price on this." The dogs looked up at him as though in agreement.

* * *

Half an hour later Harry got to his feet, albeit a little stiffly. It was still a good hour hike back down to Rose Cottage. As he looked down towards the cottage, something unfamiliar caught his eye; a reddish vehicle parked in front. He froze, trying to focus on it with his eyes, and then fumbled quickly for the binoculars, a sense of panic beginning to take hold of him. The dogs sensed the rising tension and looked up at their master, their bodies becoming rigid and alert. As soon as Harry brought the vehicle into focus he knew instantly that it had to be the red pick-up truck Michelle Compton-Smythe had seen the previous morning when he was at church. Harry picked out the word *Ford* in large white letters on the tailgate.

The front door of the cottage swung open and out walked two scruffy looking males in their mid-twenties. They were carrying Harry's grandfather clock between them. In shock Harry watched them through the binoculars loading it carefully into the back of the truck and watched them go back inside the cottage. In less than a minute they were out again, the taller man was carrying a large and valuable oil painting. It was an old scene depicting an English village pub with the local squire and other members of the local gentry riding through on their noble steeds, followed by a pack of hounds. The squire had his hat raised to an old farmer who was riding sidesaddle on a huge draught horse coming the other way.

The shorter male was carrying a cardboard box, it looked heavy, but Harry couldn't see what it contained. When they had loaded the painting and the cardboard box into the back of the pick-up truck, the male who had been carrying the box reached inside and lifted out the cup and saucer Catherine had bought for Harry, the one that had been proudly displayed in the corner cabinet. Through the binoculars Harry could see the taller man shaking his head. He watched in disbelief as the shorter man deliberately threw the cup and saucer onto the stone path. As though in slow motion Harry saw his precious cup and saucer explode into a thousand pieces.

"No!" Harry was too far away for them to hear his screams of rage and despair; they were already on their way back into the cottage for more antiques. Harry began running down the steep hill as best a man of his age could. It was a pathetic sight as he tumbled over and over, head-over-heels. Winded and in pain he struggled to his feet and tried to run again, tears streaming down his face, only to fall again. His anger overpowered his common sense, but he would not stop. He fell again; harder this time; it took him longer to get to his feet, but he was determined not to give in, the old soldier in him resurfacing. As if by some telepathic connection the shorter of the two men looked up towards the hill, in the distance he could see Harry tumbling down the hill with the two Rottweilers racing down beside him.

"Hurry up, that crazy old bastard's coming down the hill with those dogs!"

Harry pitched forward once more; he took another exhausted step forward, lost his balance and crashed headlong into the ground rolling head-over-heels, out of control down the steep slope, smashing his head against a large flint rock, knocking him unconscious. The huge gash spurted blood in a circular motion as the limp body continued to roll forwards, finally coming to rest violently against a hawthorn bush.

He lay with his feet pointing down the hillside; his jacket had been pulled backwards up over his torso, ripped and spattered with blood, mud and grass stains. Blood seeped from his head wound, flowing gently downhill along the left side of his body and on past his feet. His left boot had been ripped off by the force of the fall taking his thick sock with it. Jack and Jill could do nothing to save their master. At one point they managed to get in front of him, but he just bounced headlong right over the top of them as though they weren't even there.

The dogs stood protectively over their unconscious master, all powerful, snarling viciously. As yet, they did not know what had upset their master so much as to cause him to panic in this way. For a while they stood beside his limp body, confused and then looked down towards Rose Cottage. It was then that they saw the two men ransacking their master's home, their home. They growled deeply and together tore off down the hillside towards Rose Cottage and the intruders. In that split second the two dogs were seized by primeval hunting instincts from a prehistoric age. The only way they could have been stopped, now in full attack, was to shoot them. Even Harry would not have been able to call them off.

The dogs raced through the long grass, their sleek black and tan muscular bodies rippling as they ran, charging forwards without so much as a slip of a paw. Purposeful, two killing machines, like wild dogs racing across an African plain after an antelope. They made no sound; they did not want their prey to know they were coming.

* * *

Aware that Harry had taken a heavy fall and had not got up again and seeing the two dogs standing beside their master, the two burglars knew they still had enough time to tear apart the master bedroom and stuff their pockets with antique jewellery that had belonged to Catherine, much of which Harry had bought for her and worked bloody hard to get. Drawers were tipped upside down, their contents strewn across the bedroom floor. They turned the bed upside down hoping to find some hidden money. They tore out the contents of Harry's wardrobe, dumping the clothing into an untidy heap on the floor. In seconds the neat and tidy bedroom that Harry was so proud of had become a complete shambles. His war medals lay strewn on the floor, many awarded for outstanding bravery in the field of combat. They stepped on them contemptuously.

The two Rottweilers never missed a beat. They were not even panting when they reached the hay field, a healthy diet and plenty of exercise had them in peak condition.

The two burglars were staggering along the path carrying a very valuable and very heavy antique roll-top writing desk between them. They were about halfway between the cottage and the pick-up truck when they first saw the huge dogs. They hadn't expected to see the dogs at all, making the mistake of thinking they would have stayed with their master, giving them time to get away if they needed it. Harry was still nowhere in sight. Had they instantly dashed back to the cottage they might just have made it inside the door to safety. They hesitated for a split second and sometimes a split second is all that separates the difference between making it and not making it.

They dropped the writing desk in the middle of the path and made a dash for the pick-up truck. In their panic they unwittingly made the situation worse by rapidly closing the gap between themselves and the massive, snarling dogs barreling across the lawn at top speed towards them. The antique writing desk remained out of place in the middle of the path, as if put there as some sort of student prank.

Neither man had ever experienced real terror before; they were definitely experiencing it now. Both dogs cleared the side of the Ford pick-up truck, laden with their master's antiques, the scent of the two men having wafted across the field into their nostrils. It was the same scent that belonged to the trespassers, the ones that had been prowling around their home.

The men had almost reached the front of the truck when the dogs slammed into them at full speed. Forty-two strong teeth struck each man. The dogs wasted no time, going straight for the throats of their quarry, knocking both men to the ground as though they were nothing more than cardboard cut-outs. Neither man was in a position to scream, they couldn't, the dogs' huge powerful jaws ripped into their windpipes, all they could do was gurgle fountains of oxygenated blood as razor-sharp teeth ripped open carotid arteries, tracheas, muscles and tendons.

They thrashed about in terror for about ten seconds before going unconscious. Ten seconds of the worst living nightmare, dying slowly and painfully on a late sunny autumn morning, under a beautiful blue sky in such a scenic setting. Now their lifeless eyes stared out upon this picturesque landscape, their brains had shut down and no image could be recorded.

Flashes of blue sky, dark fur and a huge animal head tearing into their throats were the last things they saw on this earth.

Their bodies twitched for quite a while, caused by muscle spasms. Eventually, they lay still, the blood that remained inside their bodies began to drain by gravity to the areas of the body that were in contact with the ground, causing reddish pink discoloration known as lividity. In a little while rigor mortis would set in causing the once supple muscles and joints to become stiff.

A huge puddle of blood began to form around each man's head, congealing on the stone surface, some seeping into the cracks between the large flagstones. Once their hearts had stopped pumping blood stopped spurting out of their wounds. Their heads remained connected to their bodies by little more than gristle; a good sharp tug on each head would have separated them from their respective bodies without too much difficulty. The small flowering shrubs growing on either side of the path looked as though they had been painted with a fine mist of dark red paint.

The Rottweilers padded around the two corpses for a while, their bloody paws making large red paw print patterns on the stone path. In unison they turned and ran back across the field, ducking under the bottom strand of barbed wire. Having cleared the wire they exploded back up the hill in a burst of speed that would have impressed any greyhound racer, back to where they had left their master, still lying unconscious on his back in the long grass. They were like two warriors returning to camp after a successful battle, their faces and chests still covered in the blood of their enemies. Harry hadn't moved, his faithful companions began licking his face and whining, but there was no response. They stayed with him all afternoon. As the sun began to go down and the temperature began to drop they lay on either side of him resting their huge bodies against their master, their bodies helping to keep at least part of his body warm. They sensed that he was still alive and would stay with him until there was nothing left to stay for. They weren't going anywhere without him. Both dogs would lay down their own lives to protect their master, whatever the cost.

* * *

The darkness closed in quickly all around them, there was now no longer a defined horizon. Harry, in his confused state, thought he had died and wasn't sure if he was in heaven or in hell. His head felt worse than any drinking binge he had ever been on in his life, even worse than his army days. The vomit dribbled down the side of his chin and onto his neck where it made its way under his collar, congealing into a cold thick and foul-smelling mess beneath his clothes. Despite the extra heat from his dogs he was freezing, he knew that much and was shivering uncontrollably. It wasn't until he felt the familiar cold wet noses of his two Rottweilers gently nuzzling his face that he realized what had occurred and began to replay in his mind what had happened just before he went unconscious. He was so stiff he could hardly move.

"Hello, my beauties," he said in a low voice racked with pain. "Good dogs, good dogs."

Lying on the ground he recalled his unarmed combat instructor's voice bellowing in his ear from his army days, many, many moons ago. He could see the man's face on the wooden floor of the parade room, inches from his own, screaming at him, *Soldier, if you're gonna quit in here, you're gonna quit out there! Now get up and fight you lazy bastard!*

If Sergeant Pond had been lying there next to him now he would have kissed him. Harry kept remembering those words and he sure as hell wasn't a quitter, he was a fighter, had always been a fighter. Returning to thoughts of his combat days he took stock of his situation, trying to establish if he had broken anything. Hypothermia was taking hold fast and he knew that if he didn't do something quickly he was going to die out there on the hill. He envisioned the dogs staying by his body, aggressively protecting his remains from the emergency services. He didn't want to think about that scenario, it wasn't going to be a good outcome for the dogs, he knew that much.

With supreme effort Harry twisted sideways and in great pain, managed to push his upper body off the ground. He called Jack to lay down behind him for support, which the dog obediently did. He rested against Jack for a full five minutes before getting the dog to raise itself up, helping to push his master painfully onto his knees. Harry was sweating and breathing heavily with the exertion. A further five minutes went by as he rocked unsteadily on his knees, his fingers were so cold they hurt, he could barely move them. He was in serious trouble and he knew it, his age was against him now, that sheer stubborn streak that annoyed Catherine so much was the only thing keeping him going. Now that he was sweating he knew he was in even greater danger of succumbing to hypothermia, he could not afford for his clothing to get wet; that would sap the heat right out of his body in no time.

"Find my sock and my boot. Go on, away, Jilly, find it!"

Jack stayed by his master's side as his partner searched for her master's footwear. Within seconds she returned with them in her mouth and dropped them on the grass in front of him.

"Good girl. Jack, sit here boy, I need to rest against you again." Harry began to turn his body with excruciating pain so as to be in a sitting position, his body pushing against the huge dog for support. Jack hardly moved at all, pushing back against his master. After numerous attempts, Harry gave up trying to get his sock on. He had difficulty getting it on at the best of times. He persevered with his boot and eventually managed to wiggle it onto his foot. He was exhausted and sat back trying to get his breath and focus his eyes.

On any other occasion the sky would have been a picture with all the stars shining down. Because of the blow to his head, Harry was seeing twice as many stars as he should have been and none of them were in focus. Jill found her master's hiking stick, though it was now in two parts having snapped as he tumbled forward.

"Bugger! I've had that stick a long time, it's been my favorite. That took me ages to carve and varnish."

Using the broken stick as a crutch, Harry hauled himself slowly to his feet. He stood unsteadily, his head swimming, his body swaying and hurting all over. A frost was starting to form on the grass, with the wind getting stronger it felt even colder. Harry knew he was in trouble, if he didn't get moving and get warm soon he was going to die from hypothermia in full view of Rose Cottage. He'd forgotten why he had fallen in the first place and then remembered the two men ransacking his home. That made him angry; bloody angry.

"Jilly, my knapsack!" The dog searched around in the grass, running back and forth in a zigzag pattern sniffing the ground. It didn't take long for her to find it; she held it gently in her mouth obediently holding it up to her master.

"Good dog, very good dog." Harry was pleased to get it back until he heard the sound of broken glass inside and realized his thermos flask was broken. "Bugger," he said again angrily. "I've had that thermos for bloody years."

He undid the knapsack and pulled out his wet weather gear that consisted of a light jacket with hood and trousers. He was pleased to find a pair of woolen gloves in the pocket of the jacket and a woolen toque in the other and quickly put on the toque.

He stumbled back down onto the ground and yanked on his waterproof trousers. The pant legs were wide enough so that he didn't have to take his boots off. He got back to his feet using the stick as he had done before, put on his jacket, and pulled the hood up over his toque. The wind was no longer able to penetrate his clothing; he could actually feel his body warming up, except for his feet, which were still bloody cold. Even though the waterproof pants and jacket were of a thin material, they kept the wind out and the heat in; without them he would have been in real trouble given the poor physical shape he was currently in. Loosening his trousers, Harry stuffed the gloves between his thighs then thrust his freezing hands down the front of his underwear and squeezed his thighs together, rocking back and forth, whimpering in pain. Slowly, very slowly his freezing fingers began to come alive, signaled by the excruciating pain running through them as the warmer blood began to radiate through them.

"Jesus Christ!" he screamed in pain. "Come on old soldier, suck it up you big wimp, you big baby." His anger was now beginning to overcome his pain as he yanked on the warmer gloves.

No matter how much true grit he had, Harry Davidson was in such bad shape that without the extra heat, he would never have reached the barbed wire fence. He would have died insight of his beloved cottage less than two hundred yards from the comforting warmth of home and safety.

"Right then, you two, let's go and see what those bastards have been up to shall we. Okay, take it easy; I'll be all night getting down this bloody hillside."

Harry fell a few times while making his way back down the hill, but this time he made sure he didn't tumble forwards, but rather slid backwards onto his bottom whenever he felt his feet slipping out from under him. By the time he got to the foot of the hillside, his backside was black and blue from all the falls, not to mention all the mud he was covered in from head to toe. He could just make out the silhouette of Rose Cottage as he looked across the hayfield. Having crossed this field many, many times before, he had a good idea when to expect the barbed wire fence to appear. He did not want to accidently walk into it and cause even more unnecessary suffering to himself. Eventually, it appeared out of the gloom, a thin covering of ice reflecting off the strands of wire, twinkling in places like a long line of tiny Christmas lights. Harry walked along the fence line searching for the stile. He had no intentions of trying to climb through or over the fence in his condition or to even roll under the bottom strand.

Finally, he found the stile. Not without difficulty, Harry stood unsteadily on the top plank, pausing to look over at the cottage. In the dim light he was shocked to see that the pick-up truck was still parked in front of Rose Cottage. His right hand caressed the stout end of the broken hiking stick that now had more in common with an Irish shillelagh. It felt good in his large hand, he was glad he had brought it with him.

That's bloody odd, there's no lights on inside the cottage, Harry thought to himself. *Those two bastards must have got into my whiskey, I bet they're passed out somewhere inside the cottage. Just wait till I get my hands on the pair of you, I'm gonna give you a right royal bloody beating. You'll be begging me to kill you by the time I've finished with you.*

He moved cautiously towards the silent cottage, his senses heightened. He began to feel increasingly uncomfortable, not fearful; fear was not a word one would use to describe Harry Davidson. He just couldn't understand why neither of the dogs were growling. *Something is definitely not right with this picture*, he kept telling himself.

He was in stealth mode as he made his way slowly in the darkness past the pick-up truck, confused by the dark object positioned on the footpath about halfway between the pick-up truck and the front door of Rose Cottage.

What the bloody hell is my antique writing desk doing left out in the middle of the path?

Surprised he took a second look at the front door of the cottage and realized that it was wide open. He stopped and listened, only the familiar sounds that he always heard at this time of night filled his ears, the sound of a breeze rustling through the trees and long grass, the sound of leaves rustling, the scream of a fox; an eerie sound if you didn't know what it was, then the hoot of an owl. And sometimes the most disturbing sound of all, silence; that total silence when you begin to hear the sound of ringing inside your own ears.

Apart from the pick-up truck, the furniture and the wide open front door, none of these sounds gave Harry cause for concern, but he was concerned, it was that very silence that concerned him. He began to move forward again, even more cautiously this time, his eyes on the front door, then darting to the left and right of the cottage, expecting an ambush at any moment from the shadows. When his foot struck the corpse on the ground, Harry almost lost his balance. He knew instinctively that it was a human body; he had tripped over too many dead and dying bodies during nighttime raids back in a past life. Many he had killed himself, creeping up behind an enemy sentry and slitting the soldier's throat with no more concern than a business man entering an office with his briefcase; it was all business anyway, just a different line of work that was all. That part of his military background Harry didn't care to remember anymore.

He knelt down to feel for a pulse. All he felt was raw flesh and congealed blood. When he tried to move the body, he realized the man was dead.

Almost colliding with the writing desk, the toe of his left boot bumped against the second body a few yards farther along the path. He found this corpse to be in much the same state as the first one.

"This isn't good, boys. Quick let's get inside, something tells me you two know all about this," his voice was gentle but concerned.

* * *

Harry turned the dogs loose inside the cottage before entering himself, just in case he had overlooked another intruder, one who might be hiding inside and possibly armed with who knew what.

The dogs tore through the cottage together, searching every room downstairs before racing upstairs, the silence inside the cottage punctuated by the sound of deep growling. It didn't take them long to complete their search. Satisfied the coast was clear Harry cautiously entered Rose Cottage, grabbing a flashlight off one of the shelves in the kitchen before hurrying outside again to take another look at the two bodies. Jack and Jill walked nonchalantly alongside their master.

He aimed the beam over the first body and then the second. The beam from the flashlight bounced off the swirling mist like smoke in a macabre theatre production, creating an eerie backdrop. Harry felt as though he had inadvertently wandered onto the stage in the middle of the production, becoming both audience and actor. In disbelief he looked down at the grotesque bodies lying on the path. He stared at them for a long time. It was, as he suspected, the handiwork of the Rottweilers, confirmed by their bloody paw prints on the pathway. He walked over to the pick-up truck and saw his antiques piled up inside the truck bed, waiting to be driven away. Walking back towards the cottage, the beam from his flashlight illuminated the cup and saucer, smashed beyond repair on the path.

"You bloody bastards; you deserve everything you got and more!" He didn't feel sorry in the least for the two dead men. His main concern now was protecting his two dogs. He couldn't live without them if they were put down, which they ultimately would be. He needed a plan and he needed one quickly with military precision.

"Okay. Number one, hide the bodies. Number two, hide the truck. Number three, clean up the blood. Number four put everything back as it was. No, number four, light a fire, put the kettle on and then put everything back as it was."

The adrenalin was coursing through his body helping dull his own physical injuries, but he knew when he had got things ship-shape again he was going to be in a whole world of hurt. More than anything he was worried about his vision, the blow to the head had made everything look blurred and at times he was seeing double. His chest hurt so much he wondered if he had broken some ribs.

Before Harry did anything, he changed into warmer clothes, including a pair of thick woolen socks. He couldn't get his lace-up leather hiking boots on again, so he put on his green wellingtons instead. He knew that once he set about dragging the corpses into the garage one at a time he'd soon warm up, he couldn't possibly do it on his own; his strength had all but left him.

Harry reversed his Land Rover out of the garage to make room for the two bodies and for the red Ford pick-up truck, once he had unloaded his belongings from it. He then made-up a makeshift harness and harnessed the two dogs together, it was with their help that he was able to drag the two corpses across the lawn and into the garage. Satisfied, he lit a roaring fire in the hearth to warm up the freezing cottage and then put the kettle on, grabbing a handful of mixed nuts from the glass jar on the counter. They would at least give him the immediate energy he needed to get the job done.

Fighting off exhaustion Harry grabbed an old blanket and some rope. He attached the rope to a flat trolley that he used to slide himself under the Land Rover to change the engine oil. A sturdy plank was placed on the front door sill before Harry carried the trolley over to the roll-top desk. Not without a lot of foul language contaminating the surrounding fresh air, was he able to manhandle the desk onto the trolley and drag the whole thing back into the cottage. Between using the trolley and his wheelbarrow lined with the thick blanket, Harry carefully removed his cherished possessions from the pick-up truck and returned them to their rightful place inside Rose Cottage. It took him a few loads to get everything back inside the cottage and put it all back where it belonged. He picked up all the pieces he could find of the smashed cup and saucer and reluctantly put them into the dustbin.

Harry's nerves were constantly on edge, he fully expected to see headlights coming up the laneway towards the cottage, thinking the Compton-Smythes might have seen the cottage lights on and wondered what was going on. He connected up the garden hose and began washing away what blood he could see using the attached brass spray nozzle.

It was well into the night before he had the outdoor scene cleaned up. Satisfied with the job he'd done, he drove the burglars' pick-up truck inside the garage, closed the overhead door and locked it. He still had the mess inside the cottage to clear up; the floors were filthy from mud traipsed in and out. When he went upstairs and saw what the burglars had done to his bedroom he was beside himself with fury. Thankfully Victoria's painting had not been touched and remained hanging on the wall beside where his bed should have been before it got turned over. He found that strangely comforting given the complete mess the room was in. The dogs looked very put out when they discovered their bed had been disturbed. He bent painfully to pick up his medals, holding them as carefully as if they had been an injured sparrow then put them back inside his wardrobe.

Harry couldn't find Catherine's jewellery anywhere. *It's got to be in their pockets,* he said to himself.

He returned to the garage and searched the corpses for his wife's jewellery. It was all there stuffed inside their pockets. He found their wallets and removed them too; he would sort out their personal effects later on in the day. Before returning to the cottage he realized that prying eyes could look through the garage windows and see the pick-up truck inside. That would not be good. He cut open some black plastic bin liners and taped them over the inside of the windows for privacy.

"Good grief, the police will think I've got a grow-op going on here. McMaster will think I'm growing marijuana," he said quietly to himself as he taped up the windows using the bin liners.

Once the red Ford pick-up truck was out of sight from prying éyes and nosey parkers, Harry closed the garage door and made sure it was locked again before returning to the cottage, his own pockets stuffed with jewellery and the personal effects of the two dead men. Harry lovingly returned Catherine's jewellery back in its rightful place, sighing as he did so.

Finally, when Harry sat down at last before the roaring log fire with a huge mug of steaming hot tea and two thick slices of buttered toast, he noticed for the first time the blood on the faces of both dogs.

"I suppose you're proud of yourselves, aren't you? Look what a bloody great mess we're all in now. Stay there while I go and get a wet cloth from the kitchen and wipe that blood off the two of you."

Harry got up from his armchair, feeling as though his joints were seized and pried himself free, stiff and in a great deal of pain, dog-tired and irritated by what had happened. He was mad at the two men and mad at the two dogs. His slippers shuffled on the floor as he made his way back from the kitchen with the damp cloth and began cleaning up the two dogs as best he could, and then threw the soiled cloth into the fire. Before sitting back heavily into his armchair he poured himself a large glass of Drambuie.

Sitting in front of the fire he reflected upon what had happened. He knew that if the dogs hadn't got the two men before he did, he would have killed them himself anyway, of that he was in no doubt. Sipping his tea and Drambuie, he began to formulate a plan. He wanted to return to the peaceful life he had been enjoying at Rose Cottage, before the two crooks had come along and spoiled it. The dogs, seemingly unfazed by the events of the night, rested their heads on their paws and fell asleep.

Chapter Four

Harry awoke very confused, finding himself still sitting in his armchair. The sun was well up and his head hurt like a son-of-a-bitch. He staggered over to the back door and let the dogs out. The fire had long since gone out so he set about lighting another, no easy task given the condition he was in. He lent over the kitchen sink, holding on to the counter top for support, feeling dreadful. He had the urge to vomit and his vision was still out of focus from the blow to his head. He stood there for quite a while, holding himself up and swaying unsteadily, worried that he might black out. The sound of dogs barking ferociously seemed to be coming from a long way off, getting louder and louder; at the point of near collapse Harry recognized that it was his own dogs that were barking aggressively by the front door. Slowly he raised his aching head and looked out of the kitchen window.

"Oh, shit, that's all I need," he groaned.

A marked police car drove slowly up the lane, bouncing its way along the rutted track with some difficulty. Harry couldn't tell who the driver was, but suspected it was Constable Alaister McMaster. The police car stopped in the laneway just in front of Rose Cottage. Harry let the dogs out expecting Constable McMaster to get out of the car to greet them, but whoever the officer was, he didn't get out, not surprisingly because the dogs were aggressively jumping up at the driver's door, intent on attacking the occupant. Harry repeatedly called to the dogs, he tried to raise his voice, but only a low pitiful sound escaped through his parched lips. Eventually they looked over at their master and padded back towards his voice. When they were about halfway between the police car and their master they turned and charged full bore back towards the police car, with Harry cursing them, telling them to, "Get back in here, you bloody dogs," in a raspy voice, with little volume. It took a few minutes before the two disobedient dogs decided to make their way back to their master. They looked up at him defiantly, stalking past him on their way inside the cottage; not without a last minute glance back at the police car and its occupant.

Harry was dumbfounded when he saw Constable Alaister McMaster getting out of the driver's door. Normally the dogs were so excited to see him they would run around his police car barking playfully; but not this time. He watched as the officer walked up the path towards the front door. He saw him stop and then stoop down, his hands rummaging in the flowerbed alongside the path. When he stood back up he was holding something in his hand. Harry couldn't see what it was, but suspected it was part of the china cup and saucer. He shut the dogs inside the kitchen as the constable approached the now closed front door. Alaister was confused by not only the dogs' behavior but also by Harry's. It was all rather odd.

"I suppose the old bugger wants me to go around to the back door," he muttered under his breath. *What the hell's got into those dogs,* he thought as he stepped off the front porch and made his way around to the back door and knocked on it, setting the dogs off again. Harry was now standing inside the kitchen doing his best to calm down Jack and Jill, but failing miserably. He took a deep breath, composed himself and reluctantly answered the door, all the while the Rottweilers were going berserk. He creaked open the door a few inches.

"What the hell happened to you, Harry, and what's got into those dogs? Christ, what have you done to your head?"

The police officer was clutching a large piece of the china cup in his left hand with the handle still attached. Harry looked at the piece of broken china being twiddled around the officer's thick finger, he watched it spinning around and around Constable McMaster's finger, like a wild west gunslinger spinning a six-shooter. "And look at your clothes, man, they're ripped and covered in mud. You look like you've been fighting out in the field and lost."

"Fell over the dogs carrying that cup and saucer and smacked my head on the path."

"That would account for the blood splatters on the path, looks like you were washing it down too."

Harry's heart froze. "What if I was, it's a free country the last time I read the papers."

He stared back at the officer just a little bit too long before answering. Their eyes locked and in that split second Constable McMaster could feel something deep in the pit of his stomach that told him, *I don't know why you're lying, Harry, but I know you're lying.* Being able to detect a liar was something that came with years of experience, it wasn't something that the courts would be interested in; gut feelings didn't count for anything in the courtroom, but out on the street they counted for a whole lot.

"I cleaned it up as best I could. Listen my heads pounding and I really don't need any company today."

"I understand. I think you should get that gash looked at, Harry, looks pretty bad like it needs stitching. Why don't I run you up to the Cottage Hospital?"

"No! Thanks, but no thanks. I got worse in the war."

Alaister was taken aback by the sharp retort. "What's up with the dogs this morning? I thought they were going to tear me to pieces. That's not like them."

"They're having a bad day too, now if you'll excuse me."

"Yes, of course. Oh, before I go. I got a call from your landlord, Mr. Compton-Smythe, soon to be Sir Compton-Smythe I hear. He mentioned you'd been having suspicious visitors, a couple of men in a red pick-up truck. He said there might be some footprints left for me to look at."

"Not anymore, dogs churned the soil up digging for something, had to rake it all over again, damn dogs. If I see 'em again I'll be sure to call you, now you have a good day and thanks for coming."

Alaister McMaster was still talking when Harry shut the door on him. He found himself speaking to the now closed wooden door. *That was rather rude* he thought, he was a little puzzled and a bit miffed.

The officer turned and walked slowly back down the path eyeing everything he could see that appeared to be out of place, like Harry's Land Rover parked outside the garage. He always parked it in the garage overnight. Like the way the grass looked, as though something heavy had been dragged across the lawn towards the garage.

"Mm, I'm very tempted to come back later and take a look around the place when he's out walking the dogs," he muttered under his breath. "Ah, what the hell, I'll leave it for today. Harry a criminal? McMaster, you should be ashamed of yourself for even thinking such a thing."

As he drove back down the lane he just couldn't shake that bad feeling he had about, *something not being quite right.*

"Maybe it's my imagination, but I could have sworn the garage windows were blacked out with something ... Very odd," he kept saying over and over to himself. "Perhaps Harry's finally gone off his trolley."

* * *

Harry downed some more pain killers and sat at the kitchen table nursing a cup of strong coffee. He spoke aloud to his two companions lying on either side of him.

"That bloody McMaster's bound to start asking questions around the village. It wouldn't surprise me if he comes back here again when we're out, snooping around Rose Cottage like Sherlock bloody Holmes looking for clues. That would be just like him if I know McMaster. Once he smells a rat there's no stopping him. He's like a hound on the scent of a fox. Well, Harry me boy, we'll just have to make sure the hound gets put off the scent, won't we; one way or another." Painfully he raised himself off the chair, pushing the palms of his hands onto the thick wooden tabletop.

"Okay, you dogs, I'm going upstairs for a shower. I'd rather have a nice hot bath, but I don't think I could get in the bath, let alone climb out of it again, I ache so much. That was damn stupid of me falling asleep in the armchair like that. You dogs should have woken me earlier, at least I could have cleaned myself up a bit before that nosey McMaster arrived."

He let the hot water gush into the wound on his head, cringing with the stinging pain. The wound was still oozing blood after he dried himself. He dried it off as best he could using Catherine's old hairdryer and then applied a large plaster over the top of it. He looked at his reflection in the mirror, not liking what he saw.

"Ah, well, I'll probably be dead long before this wound ever heals properly. Either way I'm going to be left with quite the scar. Another one to add to the large collection you've accumulated over the years, Harry, old boy."

After letting the dogs out again he felt somewhat better and walked over to the garage to check on his handiwork, to make sure that the black plastic garbage bags he'd taped over the inside of the windows wouldn't allow anyone to peer through any gaps and see what was inside the garage, especially the prying eyes of Constable McMaster. The red Ford pick-up truck and two corpses on the garage floor would take a lot of explaining. Satisfied that nothing could be seen inside the garage and his taping job was secure, he again checked the security of the garage door to satisfy himself it was locked and couldn't be opened without his key. It was time now to implement the next part of his plan.

* * *

Harry Davidson climbed into his battered old Land Rover, and drove off into the seaside town of Worthing, as opposed to the local village, to rent a wood chipper. It wasn't unusual for him to do that, except that he normally rented one from the village hardware store. He just didn't feel like going into the village in case he bumped into Constable McMaster and he didn't want to get into conversation with the staff at the hardware store about wood chippers, especially the owner, Ray Burgess, better known as the local town gossip. He made sure not to delay leaving the laneway as he approached Spithandle Lane, concerned he might run into the Compton-Smythes. *McMaster's probably been speaking to them already about my out of character behavior. They'll be wanting to come out and see for themselves.*

As he flew by the farmhouse, he glanced out of the corner of his eye and saw the front door opening and sped off recklessly around the corner, something he never did; that alone would have them asking questions when he got back. *I've got to stop behaving like a criminal, after all I haven't really done anything wrong; I wasn't the one that killed those men. It's all a huge unfortunate set of circumstances,* he said to himself unconvincingly.

Apart from getting snarled up in the busy Worthing traffic, the drive into town was thankfully uneventful, except for the moment when a police car came roaring up behind his

Land Rover out of nowhere, lights flashing and siren wailing and then, just as Harry expected to be arrested and began to pull over to the side of the road, the police car overtook him and roared off up the road and out of sight. His heart was pounding so hard, he pulled over anyway, just to recover from the shock.

* * *

When Harry returned to Rose Cottage with the wood chipper he went inside the cottage to see to the dogs and make himself a huge sandwich of cold meats and cheese with sweet pickle. He tried not to think of the popping sound the human heads would make as they exploded out of the wood chipper in a mess that would resemble the sweet pickle now spread across his sandwich. Sitting at the kitchen table eating his sandwich, Harry wondered whether it might be better just to confess everything, because the more he delayed doing that and continued doing things he shouldn't, the more it made him look like a killer when he hadn't killed anyone. He was worried stiff that if he explained to the police exactly what had happened, his two dogs would be deemed dangerous and would be seized. There would be a hearing, the outcome of which he already knew in his heart. The presiding magistrate would order the two dogs be put down. He rationalized that would be better than getting convicted of a double murder he hadn't committed. He'd lose the dogs for sure if that happened.

He ate his sandwich without any problem at all, washing it down with a Newcastle Brown Ale. The more he thought about what those *two arseholes* had done to his cottage and to both his, and especially Catherine's possessions, the more he realized he was actually going to enjoy putting them both through the wood chipper.

Harry positioned the wood chipper in the back garden, rotating the chute to spread the flying debris over the vegetable garden. Ordinarily it wouldn't have been that difficult to slide it out the back of the Land Rover, across the open tailgate and down a couple of stout planks to the ground. But not today, though. He was in constant pain as he struggled to get the machine into position. He gathered up some brush and small logs to put through the wood chipper at the same time as the human remains, believing that a mixture of the two would help soak up the blood and help break down the internal organs and intestines.

He went into the small wood shed, lifted down his 30-inch bow saw from its nail and replaced the blade with a new one he'd purchased from town. He decided to hone the edge on his buck knife and began to sharpen the blade on the whetstone he'd left lying on the workbench. When he emerged from the woodshed the buck knife was back in its sheath attached to his belt, the bow saw was in his right hand. In his other hand resting over his left shoulder he carried a long handled axe, a tool he always kept razor sharp. The axe head was protected by a tan colored leather cover, a small strap and snap kept it in place.

This time he didn't bother harnessing up the dogs to help him drag out the bodies, instead he backed his Land Rover up to the garage door, took out a long blue polypropylene tow rope from the back of the Land Rover and made a figure-of-eight knot in the centre, leaving a loop big enough to place over the tow hitch. The remaining two ends each had an eye splice, spliced by Harry; he made a quick loop in each, bent down with some difficulty and affixed the loops around the ankles of both corpses.

Harry winced with pain as he stood up. Both corpses were lying on their backs, eyes wide open, staring up at him with cold looking eyes that now had an opaque dullness to them. Their mauled throats looked even worse, the gaping wound in their necks had opened up so large there was little flesh and bone left to hold them in place. In a brief flashback to the beaches of Normandy, he saw the faces of young soldiers dead and dying on the beach head. A brief sense of guilt and remorse washed over him.

Before hauling the bodies out like a couple of old logs, Harry spent a minute looking around to make absolutely certain there was not a soul in sight for miles around. He scanned the horizon, checking all compass points. He listened for the sound of any engine, as well as checking the sky for a passing plane on its way back to Shoreham Airport. He knew that the pilot of a small plane or helicopter flying over would have no trouble telling the difference between two logs and two bodies towed behind his Land Rover. If that happened it would only be another twenty minutes to half an hour before the police showed up at Rose Cottage. He decided that if he saw a plane he'd drape a tarp over the bodies until it had flown over and out of sight. Harry kept the dogs outside all the time he was making the necessary arrangements to dispose of their handiwork; if anyone appeared in the distance they would raise the alarm.

* * *

He was ready; his heart pounding, beads of sweat ran down his back under the plaid work shirt he was wearing. He wore old clothing, including an old pair of boots. When the job was done he intended to dispose of everything he was wearing. Harry started up the Land Rover again and slowly eased forward out of the garage, making certain not to turn too quickly in case the corpses got snagged up on the door frame. As soon as he was satisfied that the bodies were clear of the garage, he ran back and pulled the overhead door quickly down again, locking it securely. Now out of breath, not from exertion, but from too much adrenaline racing through his old body, he clambered quickly back behind the steering wheel and slowly drove the Land Rover and the two dead bodies over to the wood chipper that he had positioned at the edge of the vegetable garden. Quickly exiting the Land Rover he moved purposefully to the back of it to remove the tow rope.

"Jesus, Murphy!" he shouted. One of the heads had come completely away from the body during the short drive from the garage to the vegetable garden. Worse still, as Harry looked back towards the garage, the head was nowhere to be seen. To someone watching Harry from the back door of the cottage it would have looked as though he was dancing a little jig by the back of the Land Rover. Harry was in fact, in such a state of panic that, involuntarily his body gave the appearance of animated movement; body twisting and arms moving all over the place. The dogs, sensing their master's distress, raced over to him.

Jack looked up with the head dangling upside down in his mouth, his jaws suspending it by the gristle protruding from where the neck had once been. The dog proudly dropped the severed head at his master's feet, tail wagging. The huge dog waited in anticipation for his master to pick-up the severed head and throw it as far as he could and shout, *Fetch it!*

Harry was at first horrified, then furious, then relieved. He bent down and picked up the head. If it wasn't for the seriousness of the situation he would have laughed. The mental image of the head bouncing across the grass with Jack and Jill bounding after it seemed almost amusing. The dogs looked disappointed when their master told them both to, *Leave it!* as he tossed the head down by the corpse to which it belonged, the dogs moved in quickly as though the game was still on.

"Leave it!" Harry shouted even louder this time. The two dogs skulked away towards the laneway, giving Harry an insolent backwards glance.

In a race against time, Harry untied the two bodies, replacing the rope back in the rear of the Land Rover. *Settle down man*, he kept telling himself over and over again. Standing quietly he took a few deep breaths. A strange calmness began to settle over him. Without further thought the old man continued his macabre task.

* * *

Harry took a couple of practice swings with the axe, deftly splitting a couple of logs with surprising accuracy. Without giving himself further time to think, he turned and decapitated the other body with such professionalism that a hundred and fifty years ago he would have been hired on the spot as the Crown's local executioner. It suddenly dawned on Harry that he hadn't even tested the wood chipper, furious with himself he prayed he'd have no trouble getting it started; he didn't. The wood chipper roared into life. He turned towards the dogs and nodded in their direction. They remained like sentries standing on the laneway looking down towards Spithandle Lane, hidden in the distance by the trees. It was as though they understood their role; ready to bark a warning to their master should anyone be coming up or down the lane.

Harry grabbed one of the severed heads by the hair, blood dripping from the neck and tossed it into the wood chipper followed by a log. A spray of bloodied wood shavings intermixed with ground-up human skull and brain matter spurted out of the wood chipper, pieces of human hair sticking to the soggy mess. In went the next severed head and log, it too spurted out with the same popping sound, flying across the vegetable garden that had yet to be tilled.

Both bodies were stripped naked, a small brush fire was made and the clothing added to the fire and one shoe every so often so as not to make too much black smoke. A fire at this time of the year would not have been viewed as unusual and not a reason for the Compton-Smythes to investigate further. Harry made sure to burn anything that would identify either corpse; drivers' licenses, credit cards and photographs of loved ones never to be seen again. Harry kept the combined total of five hundred and thirty-five pounds and twenty-seven pence he found in their pockets, and decided he would mail it later to the

Sick Kids Hospital as an anonymous donation, minus expenses of course.

Had he been asked what the worst part was; Harry hoped it would never come to that of course, he would have responded by saying, *Cutting up the rest of the bodies with the bow saw and the meat cleaver that I got from the kitchen drawer was the most unpleasant part.*

Whenever he felt he was going to be sick as he set about this ghoulish part of the operation, he reminded himself of what those two scumbags had been up to. As soon as he thought about them ransacking his home, especially the dismissive way they disposed of his beloved Catherine's cup and saucer, he became enraged, after that, hacking off limbs and cutting up the torso and pelvis wasn't such an unpleasant ordeal after all.

He wasn't a psychopath, so disposing of the corpses didn't come that easily at first. Harry found the initial cutting into human flesh emotionally difficult for him, particularly the way the skin caught on the course tooth blades of the saw and the rasping sound as he cut through thick muscle until the saw blade touched bone, all of which he found quite nauseating.

The meat cleaver was a sensible last minute decision he thought, it cut through the knee and elbow joints swiftly, it only took a couple of hacks at the ankles and wrists to remove feet and hands. As each piece was severed he popped them into the wood chipper along with the small logs and brush. As he worked he was actually becoming very good at it. A couple of false alarms caused his heart to stop when he heard the dogs barking. Something in the wind had caught their attention, possibly a deer or maybe even a fox; whatever it was, it wasn't human and that was all that mattered.

Harry looked up, acutely aware that a helicopter could come flying over the tree tops and you wouldn't even know it was there until it came up over the trees. The Sussex Police helicopter had done that a few times over the years and frightened the life out of him. With that thought in mind, Harry quickly cut and split the torsos in half before heaving the bloody parts into the wood chipper.

* * *

It took Harry a good hour before the vegetable garden was covered in a good dressing of fresh human compost. There was still time for it to rot down before he sowed his vegetable seeds, planted his potatoes and dug in his tomato plants in the coming spring and early summer. His nerves were so taught with the fear of being discovered that he worked like a captured soldier, having been told his life would be spared if he got the job done quickly.

When the last piece of human flesh flew out of the wood chipper like ground beef, Harry grabbed the hose and fed water and brush into the wood chipper before turning it off and dragging it away. He then rolled out his rotor tiller and methodically went back and forth across the large vegetable garden until all was mixed in with the soil. All across the top of the vegetable garden he spread the compost he had been saving from the kitchen scraps all year, along with rotted leaves and horse manure from the farm. He would let it sit there until the spring and then rotor till the whole thing over again. Over the years he surmised, as he worked the vegetable garden and inevitably came across human teeth, he would pick them out of the soil and deposit them into a plastic sandwich bag. He would throw one out at a time at long intervals during his country rambles, hoping he wouldn't have a heart attack during this process, of course. Any wonderful memories anyone ever had of him would soon disappear when a bag full of human teeth was found in his pocket. He didn't dwell on that thought. He just didn't want Victoria pulling up a carrot and saying, *Look what I've found, Uncle Harry, oh, look I've found another one, and another one!* Before he could stop her she'd be running off back down the lane to show her mother all the human teeth she'd found in Uncle Harry's vegetable garden.

Harry tended the fire. The sound of the crackling fire and the wind blowing across the fields was all that could be heard as he stared at the fire, deep in thought.

Suddenly the dogs began barking aggressively. Harry spun around quickly, almost tripping over himself in his surprise. Coming up the lane he could see Oliver Compton-Smythe's dark green Range Rover. Oliver pulled up in front of the cottage and called out from the vehicle in his irritatingly posh voice.

"Good for you, Harry, getting the vegetable garden ready! You know how much we love your fresh vegetables. Spoke to Constable McMaster this morning, said you'd met with an accident. How's the head?"

"I'm fine, nothing to worry about!" shouted back Harry, trying not to sound alarmed and doing his best to be composed. "Hopefully knocked some sense into me," he added, trying to sound funny, but not sounding funny at all.

"Good for you! That's the spirit. Can't stop, I'm on my way to check on the property, keeping an eye out for that red pick-up truck. You haven't seen it lately have you?"

"Nope. Can't say I have," replied Harry, quite convincingly he thought.

"One of the stable lads was on his way into the village yesterday morning. According to the head groom, the lad thought he saw a red pick-up truck turn into the laneway. Best keep your doors locked, Harry, until we find what those blighters are up to. Right then, better be off. You take care, Harry!"

They waved at each other and Oliver drove off, a concerned look on his face. The Rottweilers growling menacingly at him, held in check by Harry's powerful hands on their collars.

He felt perturbed by their behavior. *They've never done that before. Better make a mental note to remind Michelle not to let Victoria wander up on her own with the dogs' recent change in temperament.*

* * *

When Oliver's Range Rover was out of sight, Harry made up a strong solution of bleach and carefully washed down the wood chipper. He then opened up the garage and washed down the cement floor with another bucket of bleach solution, hosing it down with copious amounts of water, scrubbing the surface furiously with the stiff-bristled yard brush. Harry knew from his many conversations at the kitchen table with Constable Alaister McMaster, that despite the best efforts of criminals, the Forensic Identification specialists always found traces of blood suitable for DNA analysis after a killer had washed down the murder scene. He admonished himself for not putting plastic sheeting on the garage floor first. He wasn't so much trying to hide DNA evidence in the first place, his main goal was to clean away visual evidence and return to normality, as though nothing had ever happened.

It was awkward working around the red Ford pick-up truck, but he couldn't risk driving it out into the open in broad daylight. He had considered doing it, but a little voice inside his brain told him not to risk it. He was glad he'd listened to the inner voice. How would he have explained it to Oliver? *Well, I don't believe it, Oliver, I just came out of the house and there it was parked outside my garage. The dogs never even barked.* He imagined being led into an awaiting police car, hands cuffed behind him instead of in front, after all he was a vicious killer. A mobile command centre would be setup next to Rose Cottage, forensic officers would be in and out of the house and garage, his two dogs on their way to the dog pound, assuming they weren't shot first. The place would be crawling with uniform officers, detectives and senior officers. Then the media would descend on his home. *He seemed such a nice old chap, who would have thought it,* the neighbors would be saying, clambering over each other to get their five minutes of fame. *I think the death of his wife put him over the edge; he was never right since her passing.*

Jack and Jill lay together on the front lawn, heads on their paws, seemingly without a care in the world. Harry thought it was just as well that Catherine hadn't been there to see what the dogs had done, she would have had no hesitation in calling the police, even if that meant they would have to be put down. But Catherine wasn't here anymore he reasoned and the only two real companions he had left in his life were his two dogs. Without them the future as he saw it, looked pretty bleak. Well, there was no turning back now; he was in too deep for that. He got out the pressure washer and began making a better job of cleaning the pathway. The last thing he needed was PC McMaster taking a blood scraping for DNA analysis on one of his drive-bys. *Bloody nosey cop*, muttered Harry to himself as he cleaned the path. He then made sure all trace of where he had dragged the dead bodies across the lawn was hidden by raking over the grass as carefully as he could and then standing back to see if he could still see the marks in the grass. He couldn't quite remove the tire marks left by his Land Rover, but given a few days that too would all blend in. Before returning inside Harry walked around the cottage checking for anything that looked out of place. He checked the fire again to be certain all trace of clothing, shoes, wallets and papers were now ashes and poked around with a long stick to make sure. Finally he double-checked that he had secured the garage door.

Back inside the cottage Harry armed himself with a spray bottle of window cleaner and a roll of paper towels. He then methodically cleaned the surfaces of every item he had carried back inside the house, hoping to erase any fingerprints that belonged to the dead men. They had both been wearing latex gloves when he found them, except one of them, the tall one had taken off the right-hand glove and tucked it into his trouser pocket. Harry didn't want to risk the chance that one of their fingerprints remained on one of his antiques. To be extra cautious he went around cleaning other items that had not been removed from the cottage, but that might have been touched by them. The empty space in the corner cabinet, where the bone china cup and saucer had once been, filled Harry's heart with tremendous sadness. *When I'm in town returning the wood chipper I'll look out for an identical cup and saucer. In fact I'll find a set that Catherine would have liked for herself. Yes, that's what I'll do*, he thought to himself. The rest of the day went by painfully slowly. He had to wait for the cover of darkness before implementing his next plan.

* * *

At ten o'clock that night Harry walked out to the garage. He started up his Land Rover and then went into the garage and started up the red pick-up truck and drove it out of the garage onto the driveway. He then put his Land Rover back inside the garage and closed the garage door, locking it. He got back inside the pick-up truck, pulled his cap low over his forehead and pulled up the collar of his jacket hoping to conceal his face and hide his identity. He took a deep breath and drove off down the laneway, carefully, but quickly. He felt as though he was going to be sick his nerves were so bad.

The last time he felt like that was when he and his platoon of soldiers landed on the beaches of Dunkirk; the landing craft's ramp went down and the German guns opened up. Their craft had struck a sandbank a hundred yards from the shore, he was the only one to make the beach alive, half his men had drowned, the rest had been shot and were either dead or dying. As it was, a hand grenade put an end to Harry's war. He was left for dead on the beach. The two medics that found his lifeless body argued about even bothering to take him, one feeling he was past it. The other persisted and Harry Davidson's life was saved. He would never forget that day and many others like it, though he wished he could. Even after all the years that had gone by he still had nightmares. Time was not a healer, the emotional rollercoaster was always there, the pain separated by longer periods of time instead of a constant psychological bombardment of graphic images; that was the only difference. He had coped with it better than many and that was why he was going to cope with what he had done that day and what he was going to do that night.

He prayed nobody saw him leaving the laneway, where he turned left onto Spithandle Lane. It wasn't until he was well away from the village boundary that he began to feel more relaxed. He checked the petrol gauge again; he had more than enough petrol to get him into Brighton and decided to take the north route across the South Downs by Devils Dyke. He knew this area well from all the years he'd spent living and working in the town. He had no intention of driving the paved roads all the way into Brighton. Not far from Devils Dyke he intended to turn off the road onto a bumpy track that he hoped was still there. About a mile down the winding, rutted track was a pit where stolen cars were often dumped and burnt out, which was exactly what was going to happen to the red pick-up truck Harry was now driving.

Harry pulled up beside a phone box on a secluded stretch of road, he was surprised to find that all the small panes of glass were still unbroken and the telephone still working. He phoned a Brighton taxi company. After a few short rings the phone was answered by the dispatcher. To confuse his possible pursuers, those imaginary and those real, Harry put on his best Irish accent.

"Hello, this is Seamus O'Rourke. I need a taxi to pick me up at one o'clock in the morning on Dyke Road Avenue. I'll be waiting at the entrance to Hill Top."

The dispatcher confirmed the pickup time and location. *Where do you want to be dropped off, Mr. O'Rourke,* asked the dispatcher.

"At the Ashington roundabout on the A283. I'm to meet a road crew there in the morning, but me car's broken down an all, would ya believe it? We've got a big job to do up north, that's why we're startin' early. Wouldn't do to lose me job now, would it?"

Harry remembered the pickup point from his gardening days, when he used to earn a little extra cash maintaining the grounds of the big mansion houses on that stretch of road. He would make sure to wear his collar up and to pull the brim of his cloth cap well over his eyes when the taxi came to pick him up.

Harry got back into the *borrowed* pick-up truck and drove away at a leisurely speed, not wanting to attract the attention of the police by either driving too fast or driving too slowly, eventually arriving at Devils Dyke without incident; a bleak, mysterious place of windswept green hills and deep valleys with spectacular views for miles. It was an excellent place to hang-glide if that was your fancy.

His memory hadn't failed him. He turned right onto the track that led off in the direction of the pit, winding down the driver's window as he came to a stop. He listened intently. There was nothing but the wind. The view was spectacular, he could see for miles all around. There were no car lights anywhere in sight, other than far off in the distance. Easing the pick-up truck forward, with the click of a switch he put it into four-wheel drive; he just knew he was going to need it. Halfway down the track he was glad of it, almost getting the truck stuck in a deep muddy puddle that spanned the width of the trail.

With his heart in his throat Harry bumped along the track until it opened into a clearing of brown earth. He drove into the centre and switched off the lights and killed the engine. Using the cab light for illumination Harry pulled plastic bags over his boots. At the bottom of each bag was a thick piece of cardboard, cut to the shape of each boot. He then lashed string tightly around the bags securing them to his bootlegs. He had no intention of leaving footprints at this crime scene that would match with footprints in the vicinity of his own property.

Harry Davidson stepped out of the pick-truck and removed the truck's petrol cap with his gloved hand, tossing it into the truck bed. He then took a long piece of rag from his pocket and pushed it deep into the petrol tank, leaving a long piece exposed, making sure to check that nothing that would identify him had fallen from his pockets either into the truck or onto the ground nearby. From conversations with Constable Alaister McMaster over the years, he knew all too well how criminals, in their state of heightened agitation during a crime, dropped incriminating evidence out of their own pockets at a crime scene, sometimes even their own driver's license or a credit card.

Having satisfied himself that he had made no such mistake, he lifted out the small red plastic petrol can from the truck bed. It was from his own garage. He unscrewed the cap, and doused the whole interior of the pick-up truck, as well as the truck box, pouring the residue onto the rag stuck into the petrol tank and some onto another long strip of cloth he had torn. He threw the plastic petrol can and cap inside the truck cab and lowered the windows to make sure there would be plenty of oxygen to feed the fire. He recalled the importance of lowering the windows having once come across a man who had committed suicide by dousing himself with petrol inside his car. When the unhappy soul struck the match there must have been an immediate fireball that he would have lived through in agonizing pain for a few seconds, but because the car windows were closed, the fire consumed the oxygen almost immediately inside the car and the man suffocated to death from lack of oxygen. When Harry had found him the fire was out, surprisingly there was little damage to the inside of the car or to the man. He remembered the odor of scorched pork; he'd smelled that many times before as a soldier, it was nothing new to him, it just made the taste of pork less palatable if he thought about it. Knowing this, Catherine rarely cooked pork if Harry was at home.

Once more the old man stood still, looking all around him, listening. Nothing but the wind could be heard and the beating of his own heart inside his chest, the increased blood pressure pounding in his ears. He removed his petrol soaked gloves and threw them into the cab. Then he ran the strip of petrol soaked cloth out of the driver's window, down the side of the truck and across the earth to where he stood. The petrol soaked cloth that ran from the open petrol filler cap was placed on top of the other strip, the two cloths forming a V shape with Harry standing at the pointed end of the V. He removed the cheap green colored plastic lighter from the right-hand pocket of his trousers and flicked the small knurled wheel with his thumb a few times. The spark eventually ignited. Carefully he placed the flame against the two petrol soaked cloths. Even before the flame reached the cloth, the fumes ignited, a flash of bright yellow orange flame raced across the ground in two directions, Harry raced off in the opposite direction, rolling over a small earth embankment.

Just as the cab exploded in a ball of flame that lit up the whole clearing, the petrol tank ignited and exploded into another fireball. In seconds the whole truck was engulfed in flames. Harry could feel the heat on the back of his neck as he crawled away into the relative safety the darkness offered him. He prayed that time was on his side. He knew he had to make as much distance as he could from the burning truck. If the police called up a dog unit he would be sunk for sure. He had to keep moving quickly and was thankful that despite his years he was still in relatively good shape, though he wasn't sure his heart could take the strain of tonight's antics. The handful of painkillers he had taken before leaving the cottage would have knocked out a lesser man, they had finally kicked in and he was beginning to feel a little drowsy, but at least the pain had been temporarily numbed. *Just like the army days again*, he thought. He kept heading for the bright lights of the town away in the distance to the south east of his location, mindful that he would have to cross barbed wire fences that would be hard to see in the dark.

* * *

Harry was almost at the main road when he saw blue flashing lights in the distance as fire engines and a police car were making their way rapidly to the scene of the fire. He felt pretty safe now. By the time they even got to the fire, which they would have to do on foot anyway; there was no way they could get their vehicles in there; the pick-up truck would be burnt out. While they were dealing with the fire he would be standing on the street about to board a taxi.

In the shadows Harry pulled off a small rucksack he was carrying and rummaged through its contents. He found the clean pair of trousers he was looking for and quickly changed into them, he then took off his lightweight jacket that smelled of petrol and shoved it inside the plastic bag along with his muddy trousers, making sure to tie the top of the bag tightly, hoping to cut down the smell of petrol fumes and those from the fire. He then stuffed the bag of dirty clothes back inside the rucksack. He put on the clean lightweight jacket that had been inside the rucksack and made his way down the street. At the first available bin he pushed in the muddy bags that contained the pieces of cardboard that he had worn on his boots along with the bag that contained his jacket and pants, both reeked of petrol fumes. By the time he made his destination he had five minutes to spare. He saw the taxi approaching, pulled up his collar and pulled down his cap as planned. The taxi pulled up alongside him and Harry got into the rear seat.

"Where to, guvn'or?" asked the taxi driver.

"Drop me off on the main road between Steyning and Washington, just past the turn off to Ashurst. I'm to meet a road crew there later in the morning. Ah, I'll tell you when we get a bit closer. Now, if ya don't mind I'll take a wee nap till we get a bit nearer."

"Fine with me, guv'nor. I think I know where you mean. Looks like another stolen car on fire up on the Dyke again. Bloody bastards, I'd hang the bloody lot of 'em I would. You wouldn't believe what a mess a fire makes of a car. Take my word, a brand new car set on fire the night before would look like a rusted wreck the next morning. No wonder bloody car insurance is so expensive, thanks to those bastards. Anyway, you get yourself a kip and I'll holler when we get a bit closer, all right?"

"That would be grand, thank you."

"Don't mind me asking, but what part of Ireland are you from?"

"Limerick," said Harry shortly.

"Not been there meself, my wife's from Dublin. Been there many times to see her family."

"Ah, she must be a grand lass. I haven't been back since the Troubles. Be nice to go back one day and kiss the Blarney Stone again."

"Oh, you wouldn't want to do that now, guv'nor. I hear the local youth like to piss on it for fun, you're more likely to catch a disease than get good luck."

"Is that right? Shame on them. Now if you don't mind I'll take me wee nap now. Much obliged I am to you."

Within the hour the taxi driver dropped Harry off as arranged. Harry paid the taxi driver using some of the cash he'd *borrowed* from the two dead men, tipping the man generously, but not too extravagantly, he didn't want to be remembered by the driver. The taxi turned around in the road, Harry watched its taillights disappear in the distance.

* * *

Harry new the lanes and bridle paths from the A283, northwards to Spithandle Lane all the way back to Rose Cottage as well as he knew all the scars on his own body. That was in the daytime, it was now two o'clock in the morning and almost pitch black. Every time he saw the approaching headlights of a vehicle in the distance, he would scramble into the ditch or duck down behind the hedgerows that bordered the road. The last thing he needed now was to be recognized so close to home or worse, stopped by the police.

Eventually Harry turned off the main road onto a bridle path. As he walked along in the darkness he fell into a dream. He was back in France walking along a bridle path in the darkness, alone, his friends all killed in battle. Men all sent to their slaughter. *What a bloody stupid way to fight a war,* he had thought then and still thought. *What a waste of life to fight a war anyway,* he thought. Fortunately the French Resistance found him before the Germans did.

He expected them to come now as they had done all those years ago. Everything looked the same, the darkness, the time, the landscape, even the smell of the earth and the trees. His heart began to race in anticipation. Any second now they would leap out of the bushes with rifles pointed at him speaking in French and broken English. His heart beat harder still; he collapsed to the ground holding his chest, not understanding why they hadn't come as before.

Harry lay on the ground, he thought he was dying, in fact he thought he was having, *the Big One.* He clutched at his chest, his heart still pounding and slowly returned to the present. He was back on a bridle path in Sussex, England. He was having a panic attack, not a heart attack. He willed himself to control his breathing and in turn control his heart rate, to slow it down before he really did have a heart attack. Slowly his demons left him. He allowed himself time to recover before marching onwards again, slowly raising himself to a sitting position on the path, then took out a bottle of water and a bar of chocolate from his rucksack, drank half the bottle and ate half the chocolate bar. He had to remember where the gap in the fence was that led him across the fields, through the woods and up over the big hill and down into the valley, then up and over the final torturous hill that eventually led down to Rose Cottage. Over the last few days he reckoned he'd lost over ten pounds in body weight, maybe even more than that.

He didn't want to risk going anywhere near the Compton-Smythes' farmhouse. Rex would start barking, they'd let him out and he'd have a whole lot of explaining to do when Rex found him. He didn't need that. All he knew was that he still had bloody miles to go and he was starting to feel cold. He got slowly and painfully to his feet, his body beginning to hurt again like it had after his bad fall. His head was pounding now, but Harry wasn't a quitter, he was going to make it home if it was the last thing he did. He would rest again when he reached the big hill, drink the rest of his water and eat the remainder of the chocolate, then he would slog it all the way back to the comfort of his home where Jack and Jill would be anxiously awaiting their master. He hoped they could in some way understand the sacrifices he had made for them and the enormous risks he had taken. He believed that somehow he was linked to them spiritually, that somehow they did know. He hoped that the aggressive behavior they were now exhibiting would dissipate. If it didn't, he would have to ask Oliver if he could erect a fence to keep them in. One way or another he'd find a way around the problem. A tiredness came over him that was almost overwhelming, he couldn't remember the last time he felt so old. He began to doubt himself for the first time, he was no longer certain that he would make it home, wondering perhaps if he had bitten off more than he could chew this time. His vision was beginning to blur again and in the darkness it was just another obstacle that he was going to have to overcome. In spirit alone, Harry Davidson would have made a good poster boy for today's elite *Special Air Service* or SAS as the special forces unit was better known.

The climb up over the final hill was grueling, at times Harry was on his hands and knees, gasping for breath, the stubborn old bastard just wouldn't give in. When he eventually reached the top on all fours, his spirits rose. Slowly, very slowly and in much pain he got to his feet, standing on shaky legs. His vision hadn't improved, in fact it was worse, but he was able to make out two blurred images of distant light coming from the single porch light of Rose Cottage, the light invigorated him and beckoned him homeward to a warm fire and a stiff drink. He could swear he heard the dogs barking their greeting to him, carried up on the wind, as though they knew their master was almost home and wished they were with him now. It was as though they were cheering him on.

As he descended the steep slope the sound of their barking became more distinct. It was not the barking of two aggressive dogs warding off an unwanted intruder, this was his dogs calling out to their master; letting him know that they knew he was out there and he was close to home. The sound of their barking made his spirits rise. His foot struck something hard, dislodging the object, whatever it was. He turned around on the path and faced back up the hill. Bending over he felt for the object in the grass, not wanting to risk another *arse over tit* cartwheel down the hill.

Whatever it was it didn't feel like a large stone. Now on hands and knees he groped around in the cold dew covering the grass growing on the path until his hands felt the familiar surface of his binoculars. They had been flung from his neck as he rolled out of control down the hill, just before his head struck the rock. *Maybe my luck is changing after all*, he thought. He looked through the binoculars towards the porch light, after some difficulty he managed to view the light through the lenses, however, despite his own blurry vision, the left lens was definitely more blurred than the right one, indicating that a prism had been jolted when the binoculars hit the ground. He reviewed his thoughts on the prospect of his luck changing.

All the way down the hill he remained very cautious, placing each foot carefully, it was slow going, but very necessary, his body couldn't afford to take another tumble down the hillside; he didn't need another repetition of the night before. The sound of the grass rustling and hooves hitting the ground close by, startled him as a deer raced away across the hill, about all Harry could see was its silhouette disappearing into the darkness. The wind had been in the wrong direction for the deer to catch the old man's scent as he slowly made his way down the hillside. *What a beautiful sight that would have been in the daytime, it sounded like a big one too,* he whispered under his breath.

When Harry reached the barbed wire fence he was a little off course and hadn't come out at the stile as he had expected. He was too tired to grope along the fence for it, not knowing if it was to the north of him or to the south, though he knew he wasn't far from it. Everything looked so different in the darkness. He didn't feel like trying to climb the fence or try climbing through it, instead he took off his rucksack, lay down on the grass and pushed it under the fence then he began to wriggle underneath the bottom strand, being careful not to catch his clothing on the barbs. When he reached the stone path leading up to the front door of Rose Cottage he could hear the dogs barking even more excitedly. Now they recognized the familiar sound of his footfalls and knew their master was home at last.

Harry hobbled around to the back door, unlocked it and went inside. The dogs were so excited to see him they leaped up at him, knocking their exhausted master to the floor.

"Hang on, you bloody dogs, for one minute will you! Yes, I missed you too." He pulled himself to his feet letting the dogs run past him out into the night air, while he sat on a stool and removed his boots. Wearily he climbed the stairs to his bedroom, holding the banisters tightly for support. Inside the room he removed all his clothes and put on his thick plaid green dressing gown and turned his electric blanket on high before returning downstairs with a large bundle of dirty washing. He threw it into the washing machine and turned it on. By the time he had done that, the dogs were ready to come back inside the cottage. They both lay outside the bathroom door as their master took a long and most welcome hot shower.

"All right, Jack, and you, Jill. Be good dogs. Your master needs to get to bed and take a long, long sleep. We won't be going for a walk this morning, I've done enough walking already tonight to last me a year. Just let me sleep."

Harry crawled into the luxury of his bed, warmed by the electric blanket. It felt good to be back in his bed, the coldness deep within his bones beginning to thaw under the warm covers. It didn't take him long to fall fast asleep. As usual, Jack and Jill lay together at the end of the bed. They too fell asleep not long after their master.

Chapter Five

It was after ten o'clock in the morning when Harry finally awoke. He let the dogs out again before feeding them then set about making himself breakfast. He felt as stiff as a board sitting at the breakfast table in his pajamas, dressing gown and slippers. This was unusual for him. Normally, once he was up he liked to be dressed and out of the cottage with the dogs before returning for breakfast. To him, *wearing your dressing gown around the house late in the morning was for invalids and old people or for those with no other excuse than sheer laziness.* As far as he was concerned he wasn't in any of those categories.

He heard the dogs barking excitedly and looked out of the kitchen window to see Victoria, Rex and the two Rottweilers playing happily together. At first he felt a rush of panic overtaking him, terrified that the dogs had the potential to do the same thing to Victoria as they had done to the two burglars. Quickly he opened the kitchen drawer and pulled out the carving knife; *just in case.* It was one thing for the dogs to attack and kill a couple of useless arseholes breaking into his home, but a child. He'd never forgive himself if anything happened to Victoria and would kill the dogs himself, right there and then if he had to, if they so much as hurt a hair on her head.

Victoria walked down the side of the cottage to the back door, the dogs following her. Harry had the door already open ready to greet her. She looked surprised to see him still in his pajamas and dressing gown.

"Aren't you feeling well today, Uncle Harry?"

"Good morning, Victoria. I'm a little tired this morning, but come on in. Help yourself to the biscuit jar. There's milk in the fridge, you know where everything is. I'll just pop upstairs and get dressed quickly, be down in a jiffy. Maybe we could go for a walk if you'd like?" he called back down the stairs.

"Okay. Daddy says I shouldn't come up here on my own anymore because Jack and Jill are turning vicious. They look the same to me. They wouldn't hurt anybody unless they were bad people, even I know that!"

Harry smiled to himself. When he came back down to the kitchen, Victoria was perched at the kitchen table, chocolate digestive biscuit in one hand, glass of milk in the other and a matching milk moustache.

"Well, how's my favorite fairy this morning?"

"I'm good. Did you hang my picture up yet, Uncle Harry?"

"Are you kidding? Go and have a look in my bedroom and tell me if you approve of where I've put it."

Victoria rushed upstairs, Jack and Jill hot on her heels. All was quiet for a minute, then he could hear the pine floorboards creaking as she made her way back down the stairs behind the dogs.

"Do you really like it, Uncle Harry?"

"It's the best painting I have in the whole cottage, Victoria, and anyway, how many people can say they have a painting done by a real fairy?" Victoria stood smiling by the kitchen table and finished her milk and biscuit. Harry thought how much she looked like her big sister Melanie, same cute looks, big brown eyes and freckles on the bridge of her nose. They both had their mother's looks. He couldn't help but smile back at her, pleased that she had come to see him.

"I take Wetortlire to bed with me every night, Uncle Harry. He keeps me safe and gives me nice dreams."

"Wetortlire? Who's Wetortlire, Victoria?"

"That's my beanie Rottweiler puppy you bought for me, silly."

"How on earth did you come up with that name, Victoria?"

"It was easy, Uncle Harry. I wanted something really different from everybody else. So, I sat in my bedroom and jiggled all the letters up for Rottweiler and made Wetortlire. Do you like it?"

"Well, it's certainly different, Victoria, it sounds very posh and not only that, it was very clever of you to make up that name the way you did. If ever I get another dog I'm going to come to you and ask if you would help me name it." Victoria beamed at her Uncle Harry, absolutely delighted with the idea.

"Okay, I'll grab my hat and jacket and we'll be off then. I'll walk you to the farm on the way back, that'll make a nice walk."

"What did you do to your head, Uncle Harry?"

"Fell over and banged it on a rock. I'm hoping it knocked some sense into me." Victoria giggled.

"Aren't you going to bring your hiking stick, Uncle Harry, you always bring it?"

"Unfortunately, Victoria, I was rather clumsy the other day and managed to break it, so I tell you what. Why don't we both keep our eyes open for another one this morning on our walk. In fact, let's look for a good one for you too, and when we get home I'll work on making them look really special, how does that sound?"

"I want mine to look just like yours, Uncle Harry."

"Then it will, my fairy, then it will. Did you let Mummy know you were coming up here?" By the long silence and blank look on the child's face he knew she hadn't. "Okay then, you know the drill, young lady."

"Yes, Uncle Harry." Victoria skipped across the kitchen to the telephone and called home. "Okay, Mummy, I will. Love you too."

She turned to Harry beaming. "Mummy said I can go for a walk and she said to tell you thank you."

"Okay then, let's be off shall we, the dogs are waiting."

Victoria wanted to climb to the top of the hill, but Harry just couldn't face another climb like that, it was all he could do to walk on flat ground. Instead they went through the woods, Victoria catching autumn leaves, running around like a mad thing, full of endless energy, laughing and giggling just like old times. Harry was in a lot of pain, but tried not to show it. Every time Victoria's back was to him he bent low, grimacing in pain and discomfort.

"I wish Auntie Catherine was here."

"Oh, she is here, Victoria. She's all around us. In the last few days I have felt her presence so strongly. I know she's here."

"Is she here now, Uncle Harry?"

"Yes, she is."

"I can't see her. Can you see her, Uncle Harry?"

"No, but I can feel her in the wind and in the rustle of the trees. I feel her when I see the tall grass bend over as the wind blows across it. She is with us, Victoria, you just don't know it yet. When you open up your heart she will come to you."

"I won't be scared when she comes, Uncle Harry."

"There's nothing to be scared of, Victoria. Your Auntie Catherine was always a good person and loved you very much and your sister too. She will be like a guardian angel watching over you. When you put your head on your pillow tonight and close your eyes, think of all the happy times you had with her. Don't think sad thoughts because you can't see her. Just think happy thoughts. Eventually you will feel her with you; you will smell her perfume in the air and the smell of homemade baked bread on her apron. And whenever you are sad and lonely you can talk to her and you will be able to hear her voice inside your head."

"Is that what you do, Uncle Harry?"

"All the time. Come on; let's see if we can find us a couple of good hiking sticks."

They searched the ground diligently for just the right ones and eventually found two straight beech wood branches that would be perfect for hiking sticks. Harry would later transform them into works of art back in his workshop at Rose Cottage. They walked back together through the beech wood hand in hand, carrying their treasures. These were happy childhood memories that would stay with Victoria all her life. Just her, her Uncle Harry, the three dogs and Auntie Catherine in the breeze upon her face.

As usual after he had taken Victoria on one of their nature walks with the dogs, Harry always took her home and delivered her to her mother safe and sound. He was reluctant to do so this time because of the questions Michelle Compton-Smythe was bound to ask him about the deep gash on his forehead, not to mention how thin and ill he looked. He debated leaving Victoria at the front door, ringing the bell and standing far enough away so that when Michelle came to the door she wouldn't notice the poor state he was in. He decided that walking Victoria home would be an excellent opportunity for the child's mother to see firsthand how well the dogs were behaving. When she asked him about the gash on his forehead, he would have to stick to his story about tripping over the dogs on the front path.

Fortunately, Michelle was busy teaching her weekly art class and had sent one of her students to answer the door for her. Victoria gave Harry a huge hug, she clung to him, arms tightly around his neck. Normally he would have lifted her clean of the ground, but not this time. Harry's knees buckled and he fell to his knees, gasping in pain, he was certain now that he must have broken some ribs when he took the tumble down the hillside.

Victoria screamed and ran inside the house shouting, "Mummy, Mummy! Uncle Harry's dying! Come quick!"

Michelle Compton-Smythe raced out of the house to find Harry struggling to get to his feet. She came quickly to him and gently held his arm.

"Oh, Harry what have you done to yourself you poor thing? Look at you. Tell me where it hurts," her voice was soft and gentle, full of concern and love for the old man, who was obviously in tremendous pain and distress.

Harry winced with each short sentence. "All over … I'll be fine though … had worse in the war … this is nothing."

"Let me call an ambulance, Harry."

"No, don't do that, Michelle, please, don't do that."

"Okay, then I'm driving you to the surgery."

"Just drive me home, Michelle, if I don't feel any better by this afternoon I'll call you, okay?"

"You promise, Harry. You know how stubborn you are. If you don't call me by three o'clock this afternoon to tell me how you are, I'm calling an ambulance whether you like it or not."

"I promise. How's Victoria? She had quite the scare."

Victoria sidled up to her old friend and placed a gentle hand on Harry's broad shoulder. She was sobbing. "I'm sorry, Uncle Harry, you won't die now will you?"

"Victoria, sweetheart, it's not your fault, I think you must have sprinkled fairy dust on me because I feel so much better now," he lied. "Now come on, people, get me back on my feet will you, I don't like the view down here."

Michelle helped Harry into her luxurious white Range Rover, and drove slowly back up the lane to Rose Cottage, the Rottweilers trotting alongside. Harry just wanted to get back inside the cottage. He'd made up his mind; if he was going to die, he was going to die in the place he loved, not in the back of an ambulance or inside a hospital; he was going to die in Rose Cottage.

Once inside Rose Cottage, Michelle helped Harry into his armchair and stoked up the fire.

"Here's my cell phone, Harry. The house number's already programmed into it; all you have to do is press this button. I know you won't call for an ambulance; you're just too bloody stubborn for that. The dogs are here with you, I've checked they've got water so you have nothing to worry about. Remember to call me at three o'clock. Are you sure you'll be okay, I really don't like leaving you like this? I should have called an ambulance; I shouldn't have listened to you." She bent down and kissed Harry gently on top of his head. Her voice broke. "We love you, Harry Davidson, don't die on us, Victoria will never forgive herself."

"That's why I don't intend to be dying anytime soon."

"I'm not crying because I'm sad, I'm crying because I'm angry at myself," she lied, as she petted the two dogs. They looked up at her with big sad eyes. "Don't worry, if anything happens to your master, I'll make sure you're taken care of. You can come and live with Rex. I know Oliver will say no, but he's not the real boss in the house, he only thinks he is."

She turned to look at Harry; who had fallen into a deep and exhausted sleep. Michelle watched the slow rise and fall of his chest just to be sure. She stood watching him for a few minutes before leaving by the back door and driving back down the lane. *Poor Harry*, she said to herself. *Poor Victoria too. We love that old man, damn him.*

Harry dutifully called Michelle dead on three o'clock as promised. He lied again by telling her he was feeling much, much better.

She wasn't fooled though, "I can tell by your voice, Harry Davidson, that you're lying. You're not fooling anyone."

"Michelle, I'm going to recuperate at home for a week. I promise. If I need anything I'll call you. And as we agreed, I'll phone you every morning, every afternoon and every evening until I'm back on my feet again. No visitors until then, I just want to be left alone." He sensed she wanted to say something, but didn't want to hurt his feelings.

"No, I'm not going to start drinking again, Michelle, if that's what you're thinking. I give you my word, and you know my word is my bond. I've come too far now for that. And, Mrs. Compton-Smythe, allow me to say, on behalf of the British Army Geriatric Brigade, I would like to thank you and your family for all you've done for this old soldier."

Michelle began to laugh over the phone, "Harry Davidson, you never cease to make me laugh." As she put the phone down she started to cry. Victoria bounced into the room and stopped immediately when she saw her mother's tears.

"Mummy, why are you crying?" she said gently, rushing over to her mother and hugging her.

"Well, sometimes when you love someone so much and they hurt themselves it makes you cry."

"You mean like Uncle Harry?"

"Yes, like Uncle Harry. He's been so good to us over the years. The best thing that ever happened to Rose Cottage was when Harry and Catherine came to stay. It was lucky your sister fell off her horse that day or we might never have met them." Michelle dabbed the tears away with a tissue and smiled at her daughter.

Harry downed a large glass of water and swallowed some more strong pain killers before letting the dogs out. Once they were back inside, he telephoned the rental company to advise them he needed the wood chipper for another week and then made his way slowly upstairs to bed, more dead than alive. Lying in his bed he wondered, not for the first time in his life, *This time if I close my eyes, will I ever open them again?*

* * *

Harry kept his agreement with Michelle and phoned her as arranged. She did break one rule though, the one about no visitors, she and Victoria came every day with a pre-cooked lunch and dinner for him.

At the end of five days of complete rest he was back on his feet again, though still not firing on all cylinders. Harry decided to spend the morning working in his shop on the hiking sticks he and Victoria had brought home from their walk together. He particularly wanted to turn hers into a work of art and began by carefully carving a Rottweiler on top of the stick. It was a long process, but a labor of love; it showed when the hiking stick was finally completed. It was good therapy for Harry, because when he initially opened the garage door and went to the back of the long garage where he had his workshop, the smell of bleach still permeated the air. Harry willed himself to dispel the nightmare images from his mind; he was intent on not letting the gruesome pictures interrupt his pleasant thoughts, thus spoiling his otherwise perfect day. He left the stout beech wood sticks on the bench to be worked on later before walking around to the back door of the cottage and going inside. Once inside Rose Cottage he rustled up a sandwich and a mug of tea for himself.

It was now early afternoon. Harry loaded the wood chipper into the truck bed of his Land Rover. He couldn't do it on his own, his jury-rigged block and tackle inside the Land Rover gave him the mechanical advantage he needed to haul it onboard using a couple of strategically placed planks to slide it up on. He hauled down tight on the nylon straps, making sure the machine was secure.

Harry decided, now that the current threat of another break-in at the cottage was over, the two menaces to society both now doing something worthwhile in the vegetable garden, he would take Jack and Jill with him on the return trip to Worthing. They didn't need asking twice, they hadn't been on a road trip in ages, in fact, they were so excited they yelped with joy and were almost doing somersaults. The two dogs rode up front with Harry, sitting alongside him on the Land Rover's tattered bench seat, their large heads sticking out through the open passenger window. They appeared so happy they actually looked like they were smiling. Harry pulled up in front of the rental store on the outskirts of town.

"Take care of my wheels while I'm gone, d'ya hear me?"

He didn't bother to lock the doors of the Land Rover; only a person with a death wish would try to get inside with two vicious dogs guarding the vehicle. Harry soon returned from the store accompanied by two fit young men.

When the Rottweilers saw their master walking with two strangers towards the Land Rover, they both went ballistic. The Land Rover rocked from side to side as though two heavyweight boxers were fighting to the death inside the vehicle. The barking was ferocious, the worst Harry had heard from his dogs. It took him a good few minutes to calm the dogs down, even so they continued to growl disobediently.

"Wow, mister, if I'd have known what we were going to be dealing with I'd have asked for danger money. Those are two vicious dogs you've got there, they'd tear a man's throat out in no time," remarked the older of the two youths.

"That they would," replied Harry knowingly, regretting the remark as soon as he'd said it.

"Are you sure those dogs are going to be okay, I mean, they can't get out can they?" The younger of the two youths sounded genuinely scared.

"They'll be fine," replied Harry, not totally convinced himself. His hand felt for the large commando knife he kept concealed in the inside pocket of his jacket. He always carried a knife, he didn't believe in going anywhere without it.

Somewhat reluctantly the two store assistants helped Harry to unload the wood chipper before returning to their work at the store. Harry tipped them both handsomely with some of the money he had permanently *borrowed* off the composting individuals now fertilizing his vegetable garden.

"Here's a little extra danger money," he said smiling, emphasizing the last two words. The youths looked embarrassed and began to blush as Harry thrust the bank notes towards them. No customer had ever tipped them so generously before.

"Thank you," said the older one, "but we're not supposed to accept tips from customers."

"It's not a gift," replied Harry winking. "It's danger money, remember? And you both earned it." He stuffed the bank notes into their hands, got back into the Land Rover and drove away smiling. "Well, we've made two people's day, haven't we?" he said turning to Jack and Jill.

Having dropped the wood chipper off at the rental store Harry drove towards downtown Worthing turning south towards the seafront. He was looking for one of Catherine's favorite stores; Debenhams department store. He recalled the last time he had been in the store was with Catherine. He remembered she hadn't been feeling well. His mind began to drift back to that fateful day.

* * *

They'd hardly been in the store five minutes when she'd asked him to take her home. The grey, waxy pallor of her face and the blue tinge on her lips was enough for him; he didn't bother taking her home, he found her a chair and had a staff member call an ambulance straight away. Harry remembered waiting anxiously for the ambulance to arrive, then he saw it pulling up in front of the store and the two paramedics rushing through the glass doors. The next thing he heard was a loud *thump* beside him as Catherine slipped off the chair, her lifeless body slamming onto the floor.

The two paramedics both knew that the old lady lying crumpled on the floor at their feet was dead. Out of pity for Harry standing there as white as a sheet, his eyes moist with tears, they worked on Catherine and kept working on her. Despite knowing that life was extinct they transported her to Worthing Hospital. Harry sat in the back of the ambulance with the young female paramedic. She had strapped an oxygen mask over Catherine's mouth and nose and continued administering chest compressions. He recalled the muffled sound of the sirens, suppressed by the interior of the ambulance.

Arriving outside the emergency entrance of the hospital, the paramedics whisked Catherine quickly through the large sliding entrance doors and away down the corridor, out of sight.

When Harry walked into the hospital he was in a daze; it was as though everything was in slow motion. A nurse came up to him. He recalled her saying, "Can I help you?" It wasn't a question, more a, *What are you doing here?* In all the confusion Harry had lost contact with Catherine and the paramedics. He stood alone in the hospital foyer totally lost, trying to prepare himself for the worst and at the same time praying Catherine would pull through.

"My wife," Harry sobbed. "My wife;" he couldn't say anymore. Suddenly the realization dawned on the nurse's face; the elderly woman that had just been brought in was the old man's wife.

Harry hadn't noticed the male paramedic shaking his head at the nurse as they rushed along the brightly lit corridor with Catherine on the stretcher. The nurse gently took hold of Harry by the arm and guided him to an empty room, doing her best to offer comfort to him and dreading the moment when the doctor would soon return and inform Harry that his wife had passed away.

When the doctor entered the room and told Harry that Catherine was gone, he cried out like a wounded animal. His body went into shock and he began to hyperventilate. Suddenly he collapsed to the floor; the nurse swung around and slammed the panic button to summon emergency assistance. The words, *Code Blue, Code Blue,* could be heard throughout the hospital's loudspeakers, followed by the sound of emergency staff running down the corridor.

When Harry eventually woke up he was in a hospital bed. He didn't even remember what had happened, let alone what he was doing inside a hospital. He couldn't understand why Michelle and Oliver Compton-Smythe were gathered around his bed. Never before in his life had he cried so hard and for so long when they broke the news.

* * *

These were the memories that flooded back as Harry walked into the store. He now wished he hadn't come, feeling very depressed. The bustle of people inside the store didn't help either and made him very uncomfortable.

The young female assistant must have recognized that Harry was lost in the huge store, crowded with people, barging their way rudely into one another. The only people Harry made way for were women, children and the disabled. Young men were shocked to feel the power of his shoulder when they tried to walk through the old man. The look in his eyes told them that he might be old, but he had been around the block and still knew a trick or two, so they did the wisest thing and kept going.

"Can I help you, sir?" asked the assistant, smiling broadly. She was attractive, in a heavily made up sort of way.

"Yes, thank you. I'm looking for a bone china cup and saucer. The sort of thing that a beautiful older lady would like. Something covered in yellow climbing roses, preferably with a real gold rim. Oh, the larger the better, I want to put it in the display cabinet for her. I don't want it so small that it will be lost in there."

"Come with me," she said, still smiling. "I think I have just the thing. Did you have a price in mind?"

"For my Catherine, expense is no object. Two young men were cleaning out my house the other day, one of them clumsily dropped and smashed the set we had in the cabinet. They were nice enough to give me more than enough money to cover the cost of getting a replacement."

"Oh, that was really nice of them."

"Yes, wasn't it?" smiled Harry.

The assistant, whose nametag said, *Gloria*, was more than helpful. She selected a beautiful bone china display cup and saucer just as Harry had described.

"It is made in England isn't it, miss? I don't want something as pretty as that only to find out it says, made in Taiwan or something; no offence.

"Yes, sir, it is made in England," she gave a little giggle, amused by Harry's comment.

Harry was shocked when she told him the price. He had no idea it was going to be that expensive. The thought that the cup and saucer Catherine had bought for him had cost a lot of money did not upset him. She loved him so much and it had made her very happy to get it for him. Tears came to his eyes when he thought about the moment she gave it to him, only to be replaced by anger when he thought about what had happened to it. Gloria saw the pain in his eyes though she had no idea what the cause was.

"I'll wrap it up for you very carefully," she said, moving behind the counter with the cup and saucer. "Your wife will love it. Is she here with you today? I don't want to spoil the surprise."

Harry looked at the assistant's name tag again before replying. "Well, Gloria, in a way I suppose she is." Gloria, who had been concentrating on making a good job of wrapping the gift, looked up with furrowed eyebrows.

"She died earlier this year. I just have to replace it with something she would have liked. You must think me daft."

"Not at all, that's so sweet," replied Gloria, wiping away a tear she could not stop.

"I have a picture of her in my wallet if you'd like to see it." Harry immediately regretted saying that, after all he was talking to a total stranger.

"I'd love to see it," the enthusiasm in her voice sounded genuine.

Harry pulled out his worn brown leather wallet and gently removed a small color photograph of Catherine. He had taken the photograph the summer before. Catherine was standing in the middle of the arbor; it was completely covered by an old climbing rose resplendent in bright yellow flowers. Rose Cottage stood in the background.

"What a beautiful picture of her, was this taken at your house?"

"Yes," said Harry, beaming with pride.

Harry thanked her and walked out of the store with his gift to Catherine. He didn't feel any remorse for using the money from the *arseholes* as he called the burglars. Gloria continued to stare after Harry long after he had left the store, secretly wishing she could find a younger version of him, someone around her own age.

"A penny for them," said a co-worker, and the spell was broken. Gloria began to tell her the *'that's so sweet'* story, that was soon told throughout the whole store by the end of that day.

Harry's next port of call was the Post Office. There he mailed the remainder of the *unofficially donated* money to the Sick Kids Hospital, apart from a little extra to buy himself a nice cigar, a dozen cans of Guinness and a bottle of Glenfiddich single malt scotch whiskey. *Yes, indeed; Valley of the Deer*, he said to himself, as he held up the bottle, recalling the Gaelic meaning of the whiskey.

Jack and Jill could see their master walking down the street. The Land Rover rocked from side to side as they jumped around inside with excitement. As an afterthought he decided to buy the dogs a special treat for dinner. *From the arseholes*, he told them.

"Okay, my beauties, we'll stop off on the way home so you can have a run by the River Adur. How's that? As of this moment we are going to forget all about the past week and pretend it never happened. We're going to carry on as if nothing has happened and you two dogs can start helping by not trying to eat everyone who comes to the cottage for one thing."

The drive back to Rose Cottage with the dogs was so much happier now that Harry had decided to put it all behind him. He just had to keep on working at obliterating the memory of the last week.

Harry placed the gift box on the dining room table, carefully unwrapping its contents before carrying the ornate cup and saucer over to the corner cabinet, gently placing them on the shelf where the other cup and saucer had once been proudly displayed.

"For you, my darling Catherine. Please find it in your heart to forgive me for what I have done. I miss you." He wiped his tears away then set about making himself a snack and a cup of tea.

* * *

Slowly life began to return to normal. Jack and Jill calmed down considerably after hours and hours of extra and sometimes brutal training by their master. In the end, Harry won them over, it wasn't easy, his patience was tested many times to breaking point. He did not want to kill their spirit; he just wanted them to be like the dogs he knew before the cottage was burgled. In the end he didn't have to fence them in as he thought he might have to. Despite all the training, Harry never fully trusted his dogs like he once had. He knew in his heart they were only a hair trigger away from killing again. He literally prayed that would never happen, but if it did he asked God to only let it happen in defense of himself and those he loved. He would justify his prayer by telling himself, *God moves in mysterious ways, Harry.*

Christmas arrived, this year it was a white Christmas, but that wasn't unusual as the seasons became more fickle. Rose Cottage, her thatched roof covered in snow looked like an artist's dream. Harry still received royalties from the various photographs he had submitted. Now the beauty of Rose Cottage during all four seasons could be enjoyed by the public as they bought postcards from the local village shops. One year the cottage appeared in a calendar depicting picturesque rural scenes of Sussex.

This Christmas, Harry had been invited down to spend Christmas Day at Saxon House with the Compton-Smythes. He really didn't want to go, but once he crossed the threshold he was glad he had made the effort. He stayed for lunch, thoroughly enjoying the roast pheasants, they must have known they were his favorite, no doubt Catherine had mentioned it to Michelle at one time. Harry was as thrilled to see Melanie as she was him. Law School was going very well for her.

"When I do become a lawyer, Uncle Harry, I am going to take care of all your legal requirements pro bono publico. But, of course, you will never need the services of a lawyer anyway, Uncle Harry, because you are such a pillar of society, an all round good person."

Harry flushed with embarrassment and guilt. "Melanie, no mortal being is a saint, not even your Uncle Harry, I'm sorry to disappoint you. However, should the time ever arise that I need a good lawyer, you can be certain I shall be retaining your services, provided I am a paying customer. You won't get very far not charging people you know."

"I will hold you to that, Uncle Harry," replied Melanie naively. "If everyone was like you, Uncle Harry, law practices would go out of business."

Harry felt his stress level falling when the subject changed from Harry Davidson's saintly existence to the world's changing weather patterns. He fully expected someone to ask him what criminal acts he could have possibly committed in his lifetime. He didn't think he could keep his composure if that statement had been made.

After a magnificent Christmas lunch, Oliver passed the decanter of port around the table to his many guests. Sitting next to Harry on his left was the chief constable of Sussex, to his right, the vicar, Angus McCreevy. The newly appointed mayor, Chuck Wilson, was also there along with some of Michelle's *artsy* friends. Harry had no trouble fitting in at such auspicious occasions. His great wealth of horticultural knowledge made him a great favorite, especially among the ladies. He was quite a character and fun to be around, particularly after a few glasses of *wobbly pop.*

Oliver raised his glass. "A toast. To all my good friends and family gathered here today, God bless you all. Here's to health and happiness and many, many more Christmas dinners together. And finally, to absent friends!" A resounding, *Here! Here! To absent friends!* echoed around the huge stately banquet hall, filled with many famous people and dignitaries. Harry recognized some big names in the business world, one in particular had been interviewed on the BBC program Panorama, but he couldn't for the life of him remember the man's name.

* * *

Harry decided to see the New Year in at the village pub, taking a taxi there and arranging for one to return him home as soon as the New Year was rung in. He didn't want to be alone at home and didn't want to spoil his relationship with the Compton-Smythe's by making them feel sorry for him, and feeling they had to invite him to every event on the calendar. He knew it would be a raucous occasion at the pub and he actually looked forward to it. He surprised himself by taking his harmonica with him, knowing that the singing and merriment would be well underway by the time he got there.

The snow was falling heavily, a reminder that winter was well entrenched. Harry struggled into his heavy winter coat, pulled on his woolen toque and mitts, stuffed his scarf into his coat pocket and grabbed his hiking stick. The taxi might just make it up the lane, but it certainly wouldn't make it back down, judging by the way the snow was piling up in the laneway.

Looking out through the lounge window he was satisfied that his assumptions were correct; he patted both dogs on the head and opened the back door. When they saw the snow driving hard across the field by the gale force winds, they returned to the comfort of the fireside. Harry checked his pockets for his torch and compass, fully aware how dangerous it was to be caught in a whiteout. Many had perished just yards away from safety because they couldn't see where they were going and had completely lost their sense of direction only to be found frozen to death a stone's throw away from their homes.

"See ya later, ya big babies," were his parting words to his companions. Then he stepped out into the freezing night, feeling invigorated as he struggled down the lane to meet his ride at Spithandle Lane.

"Christ, Harry, you retired from the army years ago. Do you have to make everything in life so hard, as though you're on a constant military exercise?" shouted Paul, the taxi driver. "Quick get in," he said above the roaring wind and swirling snow. "I almost called you to abandon the mission myself, but then I remembered what a stubborn old bastard you are. I knew if I wasn't here to get you, you'd bloody well trek through the snow all the way to the Whippletree, even if it killed you."

Harry smiled, "That I would have done, Paul, that I would have done. Done it many times before, traipsing through the Canadian Arctic on army maneuvers. This is nothing boy."

"Yeah, I'm sure you have, Harry, but you were probably, what, nineteen at the time? If this keeps up we'll both be building a bloody igloo to share."

"Done that too," replied Harry with a grin, unconcerned by the appalling weather conditions.

After some heart stopping moments for Paul, narrowly avoiding putting his vehicle into the ditch, they arrived outside the front of the Whippletree just after eight o'clock New Year's Eve. The rural pub was situated about halfway down the village high street. Harry gave Paul, a man whom he knew very well, strict instructions, on pain of death to collect him twenty minutes into the New Year.

"Harry, my taxi's staying parked outside, I'm not going anywhere tonight, other than to try and get you home. We'll see the New Year in together and don't worry, I never drink and drive, I value my license too much, not only that, my wife would kill me."

As soon as Harry walked inside the Whippletree, both bars, lounge and public alike erupted with cheers and warm welcomes for the old man. He was treated like a celebrity and no one would let him dip his hand into his pocket to pay for a drink all night.

Once Harry had been accepted back into the bosom of the establishment, a young fellow, with an outstanding voice broke into song, singing, *I've been a wild rover for many a year ...* whereupon, the entire pub erupted into song. Another patron began playing the honky-tonk piano, someone shouted, *Come on, Harry, play a tune on your harmonica, we know you've got it with you!* Others pleaded with him to play, and so he did. A guitar was being tuned and then a fiddle, the whole place was in full song and remained that way right through to *Old Langsyne*.

It was nearer to one o'clock in the morning when Paul helped a very inebriated Harry Davidson into his taxi. Harry had an arm draped around Paul for support. The snow was falling lightly now, though the roads had already received a thick carpet of snow. The drive back home to Rose Cottage was even more dangerous than the ride in. Harry sat in the front passenger seat, suitably sloshed and with a silly grin on his face. Harry wouldn't let Paul drive him from

Spithandle Lane to the cottage. The taxi would never have made the first ten yards up the lane; the snow was, by now, too deep. Harry had been one happy drunk that Paul, apart from the slippery conditions, had pleasure driving home.

"Well, Harry, we're gonna have to footslog it all the way back to Rose Cottage together."

"Nah, I'll be fine, Paul, just watch me. Safe drive home, lad." Harry turned and did a face plant into a snow bank.

Paul was a veteran of the Falklands War and wouldn't take *no* from a fellow soldier. He helped a giggling Harry out of the snow bank, brushed the snow off him and placed Harry's right arm over his shoulder. Together they struggled through the deep snow. Paul was amazed at the determination and strength of the elderly man he supported.

The two veteran soldiers, a generation apart in age laughed and joked all the way back to Rose Cottage, stumbling up the lane through knee-high deep snow, at times it was up to their thighs. On more than one occasion Paul had to pull Harry out of a snow bank. The two men would struggle to their feet laughing hysterically, hugging each other, an embrace that no other human being could understand unless they had seen combat. Paul refused to accept payment from Harry on the return trip, not even a tip. Harry embraced Paul again in another drunken bear hug, told him he loved him for being such a

Christian and staggered inside Rose Cottage. The dogs were pleased to see him, no matter what state their master was in.

Paul helped his friend into the armchair, threw some more logs onto the fire and with much tugging managed to yank Harry's winter boots from his feet. Jack and Jill were never far away, growling occasionally. They soon realized that Paul, whom they knew, was trying to help their master and make him as comfortable as possible. Before leaving the cottage, Paul covered a now snoring Harry with a thick green tartan wool blanket.

As Paul was about to open the back door to leave and struggle back down the lane to his taxi, Harry looked up, smiled and said, slurring his words, "Why couldn't women be more like dogs sometimes? It doesn't matter what you do, where you go, how long you're out, when you get back, what state you're in when you get back, dogs are always pleased to see you. I remember a conversation I had with Catherine many moons ago, she was getting frustrated with me over something. I can't remember what it was now, anyway it doesn't matter. She said, *You know, Harry Davidson*. She always called me *Harry Davidson* when she was mad at me. *You know, Harry Davidson*, she said. *Sometimes I think you love those dogs more than you do your own wife*. I thought about that for a moment and replied, Catherine, my darling, if I shut you in the boot of the car with the dogs for an hour, who do you think would be the most pleased to see me when I got back and opened the boot an hour later?"

"And how did that go over, Harry?" laughed Paul.

"Well, Paul, let's put it this way. I don't recommend you pass those words of wisdom onto your wife when she's mad at you."

Paul smiled at his friend and closed the door behind him then began the long struggle through the thick snow back down the lane to his taxi. All the way he kept thinking about Harry's parting words. He was still laughing when he finally arrived at his own house.

Harry meanwhile could see himself standing in front of Catherine with a mischievous grin on his face, and Catherine saying, *Harry Davidson, sometimes you are impossible. It's just as well I married you, no other woman would put up with you.*

Harry burst out laughing, the mental image of raising the car boot to one pissed off wife and two dogs wagging their tails excited to see him, always struck him as comical, but no matter how mad Harry made Catherine, when he smiled at her with that mischievous grin of his, she just couldn't keep mad at him for long.

With enormous difficulty and a few tumbles to the floor, plus both dogs jumping all over him with excitement, Harry eventually got unsteadily to his feet. He threw a few more logs on the fire, drank two huge tumblers of water and sank into a deep sleep slouched in the armchair in front of the fire, clumsily pulling the thick tartan blanket over himself. Jack and Jill lay down between the fire and their master; they too were soon asleep, woken occasionally by Harry's snoring.

Chapter Six

January was particularly cold and blustery. Harry went on about his business at Rose Cottage and the world went on around him.

Constable Alaister McMaster was sitting in the small report writing room at the village police station, twiddling the broken china cup around his finger. On a whim he drove to Brighton Police Station to speak to Erin Scott, a Scenes of Crimes officer he respected and trusted. It was his day off, but he was able to convince his wife Jen that they could go shopping in Churchill Square or Western Road, or afterwards, both if she liked. Jen wasn't too thrilled at her husband dropping into any police station on his day off, but she loved him and if he felt it was important then she could forgive his quirkiness.

As he jumped out of the car on John Street, Jen shouted, "Give Erin my love and tell her it's about time we had another girls' night out!"

"I will!" he shouted back. He hadn't gone ten paces when he remembered he had left the evidence bag in the car.

"Forget something again, Officer?" Jen held up the bag for him. "Good job you're retiring soon, darling, and you've got me to look after you."

Alaister smiled and kissed her. "As long as I never forget how lucky I am to have you."

"You better not, unless of course you want to give me half of everything."

Alaister wasn't sure why he wanted Erin to examine the china cup fragment for fingerprints, he wasn't convinced it was necessary, but he just couldn't shake the nagging feeling he had, it just wouldn't go away. At times he found himself waking in the middle of the night and on his day off too thinking about it. He felt a little guilty that he was asking her to do this for him and was probably wasting her time, especially knowing how overwhelmed with work she was. Erin was one of those rare individuals for whom, nothing was too much trouble. She had great respect for Alaister, not only as a police officer, but also as a person. They were very good friends on and off the job.

"Is it urgent, Alaister?" Erin asked.

"No, it's just a hunch I've got. Let's not bother submitting it officially, unless you find something that is, I don't want to waste your time, I know how busy you are."

"Okay, Alaister, just don't let the bosses hear you say that. You know they have that directive on submitting evidence to SOCO," she admonished. "I won't be able to get to it today, but first thing in the morning I'll take a look at it. Are you on tomorrow morning?"

"Unfortunately I am."

"Okay, if I lift something I'll say you gave it to me officially now, if I don't find anything, what do you want me to do with it?"

"Call me on my cell phone if you find something, if not, send it to me through the courier. If you do find any prints they'll probably be the owner's anyway."

"Is the owner on file?"

"Not the last time I ran him, as clean as a whistle."

"What's it about anyway, Alaister?"

"Just a nagging feeling I've got that won't go away."

"Oh, right," she smiled. "The *Detective Alaister McMaster* gut feeling. I can't wait to see your cross-examination in the box on that one. Okay, Sherlock Holmes, leave it with me."

Alaister dropped the piece of china cup back into the brown paper evidence bag and handed it to Erin. "Thank you, Watson."

"You owe me," were her parting words as Alaister walked through the swing doors. She liked Alaister *owing her* because it meant another lunch date at the pub at his expense.

The following morning Erin Scott lightly dusted the fragment of china cup with black fingerprint dust. As she did so, two clear latent prints appeared on the surface. Even with the naked eye she could see that the ridge detail was excellent. She began to take photographs of the fingerprints, at first without any scale and then with a small paper scale next to each print.

Before going any further she phoned Communications and asked them to have Constable McMaster call her A.S.A.P. She took the interval to enjoy her cup of coffee as she waited for the officer to call her back. Conscious of her weight, she decided not to buy a muffin at the coffee shop on her way to work. She couldn't understand why men found her attractive, but they did, probably because only she saw herself as overweight. The telephone rang returning her mind from its wanderings to the task at hand.

"Alaister?"

"Hi, Erin. I thought you might call me on my cell, wishful thinking I suppose. I guess you didn't find anything. You want me to come by and pick it up or do you mind sending it through the courier?"

"Actually, I have two good prints, but I'm not going to lift them until I have an incident number. Do you still want me to go ahead with this?"

"Sure, let's see what they reveal."

"Okay, then I'll submit them, as it's not urgent it could be a few weeks before I hear back."

"That's okay, Erin, and thanks. Oh, I'll get that incident number for you and call you straight back." Within minutes Alaister called back with the number. Now Erin could get on with the job, *officially* this time.

Erin placed another small label with the incident number, the date, her badge number and a small arrow to show the position of the print on the fragment. She then took another series of photographs. She placed a piece of white plastic board on top of the laboratory table, on top of this she carefully taped the two edges of a white fingerprint card. Having done this she cut a length of special fingerprint tape that she was going to use to cover the two fingerprints. Because of their position on the cup fragment, she was able to lift the two prints together. Now came the tricky part.

Very carefully Erin smoothed the tape completely over the fingerprints, being careful not to leave air bubbles under the tape. She took a deep breath and slowly removed the tape, as she did so the dusted prints came up on the tape perfectly, along with the small identification labels and scale. She transferred the tape to the white fingerprint card, starting at one end and began to gently smooth the tape over the card, again making sure there were no air bubbles. Erin looked at the two prints expertly positioned on the card, the ridge pattern on each almost perfect. She made a quick sketch on the other side of the card and filled in the details before submitting it to the NAFIS[1] coordinator. Having done so, she got on with her other pressing work

---

[1] *NAFIS: National Automated Fingerprint Identification System.*

and didn't give Alaister's submission another thought.

It was three weeks to the day when Erin Scott received the news from the NAFIS coordinator. She'd been off sick for a couple of days when the news broke. When she got to work there was a brown envelope on her desk addressed to her. She opened it and pulled out the printout with the information. The fingerprint match was identical to James McMahon, one of two men on the Sussex Police most wanted list of criminals, the other was Justin English, McMahon's accomplice. Erin could not believe what she was looking at. There on the paper before her eyes was one of two men she hated with all her heart. Two men who had constantly eluded capture despite the very best efforts of police forces across the British Isles. She sat back in her chair, her mind returning to that awful day.

* * *

James McMahon was one of two men wanted for a series of armed robberies, rapes and burglaries across the United Kingdom. One involved the brutal rape of a young housewife who had arrived home from work a little earlier than expected. As she unlocked the front door and walked inside her house, she had no idea that two men had broken in through the rear kitchen window and were now upstairs in the master bedroom pocketing her jewellery. They froze as soon as they heard her pushing the key into the front door lock. Within seconds the items they had spilled onto the queen-size bed, were swept underneath the top quilt. They crept silently across the bedroom and waited behind the door. Melissa Markham took off her coat and hung it in the hallway cupboard before climbing the stairs to the master bedroom.

As she made her way up to her bedroom she smiled to herself, pleased with the way she had decorated the house. The house was immaculate. She was very proud to be a young housewife.

Without thinking she walked into the bedroom and froze, something was out of place, *Ah, yes, the quilt*, that was when she felt a presence behind her. Before she could react a hand was placed forcefully over her mouth. She tried to scream and kick out, but her legs were lifted off the floor, she was carried the short distance to the bed, falling onto her back, her long blonde hair splaying over the pillows, the hand still over her mouth, but with the attacker now in front and on top of her.

Jimmy McMahon held up a large knife in his free hand, placing the flat of the blade across her right cheek. Melissa looked up into her attacker's face, her bright blue eyes full of terror. The second intruder, Justin English, began pulling down her tights and panties, she kicked out, her high heel shoes banging off the ornate white dressing table. McMahon tore open her blouse and cut through her bra. Tears streamed down Melissa's face, leaving trails of black mascara down her cheeks. McMahon covered her mouth in duct tape and with the help of English, began his brutal rape of this lovely young school teacher.

McMahon was twenty-six years old, six foot two and two hundred pounds. He loved watching people suffer; he was a man that always picked his fights, a despicable creature. His sidekick, Justin English, twenty-two, was five feet seven, one hundred and sixty pounds and did whatever McMahon told him to do. McMahon was his hero. He was so excited watching McMahon raping the young housewife that he came in his own pants. When it was his turn, he couldn't get it up and felt belittled in front of McMahon. His lust turned to rage, he was so angry and humiliated that he beat the young woman savagely with his fists.

When McMahon saw the small photograph on the bedside table of the woman's husband standing proudly in his policeman's uniform, he told English to, *Hurt her some more and make the pig-bitch squeal.*

English finally stopped punching Melissa, not because he wanted to, he was just too exhausted to punch her anymore. They left her unconscious body sprawled on the bed.

Melissa's blood had spattered across the walls and ceiling as the thug's bloodied fists were drawn back and forth, hammering into her face like pistons. McMahon was later identified from a DNA swab taken from the woman's vagina as well as from a large scar on his right forearm. The scar was from a police dog, a German shepherd called Bob. An unassuming name for such a vicious dog.

McMahon had been running away from a previous burglary and wouldn't stop to the commands from the police dog handler to, *Stop or I'll let the dog go!* So the officer let Bob go and Bob liked to go. He loved to run down his prey and loved it even more if they fought back, that only made him more aggressive.

He took Jimmy McMahon down in one leap, holding onto his right arm. Jimmy struggled on the ground and made the mistake of fighting back, punching the dog repeatedly in the head. Bob exploded into rage and tore at the arm inflicting serious damage. His handler had to literally pull the dog off the man, using all his strength to stop the dog going in for a second attack. Since then Jimmy McMahon both hated and feared big dogs, especially police dogs.

Melissa was later able to recall the huge scar on her attacker's arm, but that was a long, long time later after reconstructive surgery to her broken face and even longer psychological counseling. The Sussex Police believed that McMahon's accomplice in the rape was Justin

English, another one of life's losers. He had left no DNA evidence that the forensic team could find, but Melissa, without any hesitation, had been able to pick him out of a photo line-up.

McMahon and English turned their criminal minds to terrorizing banks and convenience stores up and down the country. Their attack on Melissa had been among one of their most brutal rapes.

Both men were suspected of a number of female abductions, none of the women were ever found, their broken bodies dumped, in as yet undiscovered make-shift graves. Perhaps they would never be found. The pain and untold suffering for families, friends, loved ones and coworkers was a legacy of eternal mental anguish.

* * *

When Melissa did not return to school after her lunch break, the school secretary kept phoning her house. The Principal reluctantly telephoned the police and a, *Check on the wellbeing* call was generated. A two man unit sped to the house, emergency lights on the whole way, siren wailing where necessary. Everybody liked Constable John Markham and until the two officers on their way to his house knew his wife Melissa was okay, they weren't taking any chances. This was a brother officer's wife.

When they discovered the broken kitchen window at the back of the house the officers called for other units to attend. At this stage they didn't know the intruders had left through the front door.

McMahon and English walked calmly down the street, carrying two sports bags stuffed with jewellery, cash, liquor and CD's. So as not to draw unnecessary attention to themselves, they drove their stolen Ford Cortina sedately away, making sure not to speed and to obey the Road Traffic Act.

Once a police perimeter had been set-up around the house, the first two officers to arrive entered the house through the open kitchen window, making their way quietly upstairs. As they neared the top of the stairs they could hear the sound of someone moaning from one of the rooms. The leading officer swung open the bedroom door and gasped when he saw Melissa's battered, naked and bloodied body on the bed, blood spatters up the wall and across the ceiling.

"Get an ambulance here now!" he screamed into his radio. "We have an unconscious and severely beaten female. She needs urgent medical assistance!"

Within minutes the sound of sirens could be heard in the distance, getting louder and louder as an ambulance and police cars sped towards the Markham's house. Yellow police tape soon surrounded the house. Detectives and forensic officers descended on the Markham home, one of whom was Erin Scott, also a good friend of the Markham's. She was soon dispatched to the hospital to take photographs of Melissa's injuries and to take custody of the sexual assault kit, once the medical staff had released it to her. She would ensure its speedy delivery to the forensic laboratory where a DNA profile would hopefully be developed.

Bad news travels like a tsunami throughout a police department and the Sussex Police was no exception. Constable John Markham had just been assigned to a plain clothes street crime unit. As yet he had not heard the terrible news. When his detective sergeant called him on the air, requesting he return to the station immediately, John argued with him, he was about to make a big drug arrest. The words, *Sod the drug arrest John, get back here now! Melissa's had an—an accident.*

It wasn't long before his best friend Alaister McMaster got the news. At times his patrol car was completely off the ground as it hit the occasional dip in the road. Alaister wasn't even looking at his speedometer as he raced to the hospital, lights flashing and siren wailing non-stop all the way. When he entered the hospital emergency wing his car was doing a four-wheel drift across the car park, stopping sideways next to the emergency doors. Alaister was out of the car and running.

Alaister's wife Jen had called him from the hospital; she was one of the RN's on duty in

Emerge when her unrecognizable friend Melissa was rushed in through the doors by the ambulance crew. She was all business when Alaister got there. This was not the time for tears; she would have her break-down later. First she had to help save her friend's life.

Alaister took one look at his wife's face and knew Melissa was in bad shape. John burst through the doors as distraught as any human being could be, to the point of being out of control. Alaister rushed to comfort his friend, but John reacted completely out of character, all he saw was someone in his way, blocking the path to his injured wife. He punched the figure in front of him hard in the face. Alaister fell back, crashing to the floor. As John stepped over the fallen officer, part of his brain registered the uniform and he looked down. Jen came straight to John, his needs were more urgent than her husband's. Alaister's black eye would heal; John's broken heart might not. As Alaister slowly groped his way to his feet, his wife and John Markham had already disappeared through a set of swing doors on their way to the intensive care unit.

An hour later Jen returned to the ward, she slipped her hand inside her husband's arm and together they walked outside without a word. Under the shadow of an adjacent building, Jen buried her head into her husband's chest. Her first sob was a gentle whimper, and then the flood gates opened. He pulled her in close to him, his chin on top of her head, one hand gently caressing her back, the other holding onto the back of her head. He tried to talk soothingly to her, but his mouth felt so tight, he was trying not to cry himself, trying desperately to be the strong one. Finally he succumbed to his own emotions. They stood there holding on to each other sobbing into each other's arms.

They walked back inside, their eyes red with tears. Jen led her husband through a series of doors and long brightly lit corridors to the ICU ward. John stood up and embraced his close friend and colleague.

"What happened to your eye, Alaister?" he asked through tears of rage, truly oblivious to the fact that he was responsible."

"It's nothing, John, how's Melissa doing?"

"The doctors don't know yet, they don't even know if she's going to make it, Alaister." John sank back down on the chair, placed his head in his hands and wept uncontrollably. Suddenly he sprang back out of the chair in rage, "I'm going to find whoever did this to my wife and kill them with my bare hands. I'm going to torture them so bad they'll be begging me to kill them!"

"John, John, I'm Doctor Reynolds. I need to talk to you." The Doctor placed a comforting hand on the big man's shoulder. John looked over at Jen and Alaister.

"They're like family to me, Doctor, I need them with me if that's okay?"

"Of course it is. John, because of the severity of your wife's injuries I'm having her airlifted to a London hospital, there's a lot of facial reconstruction to be done. John, she's in critical condition. I know you're angry, but you need to put all your energy into helping your wife. She needs you right now. For the moment, let the police handle what needs to be done. There won't be enough room in the helicopter for you I'm afraid, I need a medical team with her at all times. John, please don't give up hope, we're doing everything we can and more to pull her through this. You need to be strong. Okay, enough said. Jen, Sister's got the details." Doctor Reynolds turned to go. "Oh, Jen, I've spoken to Sister, as of now you're off the ward. Go and be with your friend." Jen looked at the doctor in surprise, not fully comprehending what he was saying. "There's no argument, Jen. In fact as far as I'm concerned you're on the flight team. Hurry up, Nurse, go and get ready!"

Jen hugged John and Alaister and took off up the hallway running. Alaister received a message to call Communications straightaway. When he got off the phone he nodded to John. "The chief constable has authorized a traffic car and driver at your disposal twenty-four-seven. As of now I'm on leave. Come on, mate, our police chauffer is outside waiting for us"

Many believe, without justification that they are good drivers, but until you've sat as a passenger in a Sussex Police Traffic car driven by an experienced traffic officer, you don't know what good driving is. Such was the experience for Alaister McMaster and John Markham. They were driven lights and sirens all the way to London at high speed, never once did they feel unsafe in the hands of their expert driver.

As they were flying up the M23 motorway, Alaister turned to John and whispered, "It's the white silk scarf the traffic guys wear that does it." John never heard, his mind was miles away, willing his wife to live with every living cell within his own body.

* * *

That whole week had been a blur for all of them. Once *SOCO* had finished with the crime scene, Alaister and some of his colleagues went back to John and Melissa's house. They cleaned the blood off the walls and ceiling in the bedroom, tore up the blood-stained carpet, repainted the walls and ceiling and finally laid a new carpet. The broken window was also fixed. Everything was done to prepare the house for sale. John and Melissa Markham would never be coming back to it again. The Sussex Police Association paid the bill with many donations from other police officers coming in from across the country to help the couple. Alaister dumped the bed and mattress. *SOCO* had already seized the pillow cases, the pillows, the sheets and the quilt. What they needed from the mattress had already been cut out.

When Alaister finally heard the news about what had happened to his friend's wife, his rage was uncontrollable, he was hell-bent on going on a killing spree of his own. As far as he was concerned, when you hurt a police officer's family, there were no rules. He'd devoted much of his time on and off duty trying to find the two bastards that had almost killed his best friend's wife. He never discussed what he was doing with anyone, constantly reminding himself of an infamous motorcycle gang motto, *Three can keep a secret if two are dead.*

* * *

Erin sat back up in her chair shaking, the printout still in her hand, tears in her eyes. She rummaged around on her desk for Alaister's schedule and saw that he had the day off. She knew he wouldn't mind receiving a telephone call at home from her. *He'll be jumping for joy,* she thought as she dialed his home number, unable to contain her excitement.

When Alaister answered his phone, Erin had trouble containing her emotions.

"Have I got some great news for you, Sherlock."

"You've won the lottery?" replied Alaister nonchalantly.

"Even better than that, my friend. Those prints I lifted for you, they belong to none other than Jimmy McMahon! Who's a clever boy then?"

"Yeah, I heard Erin, good work too. Listen this isn't a good time to talk, if you get my meaning." Erin sensed the strain in his voice.

"Alaister, is there something you're not telling me?"

"No, Erin, everything's fine."

"Come on, Alaister, it's me, Erin, remember." There was a long silence. "You can't talk can you?"

"I'm sorry, Erin, it's better this way. You're not in any trouble. I submitted the item to you and you lifted the prints, that's all that happened. That's all you need to tell them."

"I see." Erin took a deep breath and exhaled. "Okay then, Constable McMaster, you take care."

Erin replaced the receiver slowly, confused and worried about her friend. His stilted conversation and matter-of-fact tone gave her cause for concern. *They've tapped his home phone. Oh, Alaister, you're really in the shit this time. There's no doubt those bastards from Professional Standards are involved in this one.*

* * *

"Sit down, Constable McMaster." Chief Superintendent Bernie Robertson, officer in charge of Horsham Police Station was Alaister's boss. "This is Detective Inspector David Quinn. I think you two know each other." Alaister looked at Quinn, unable to hide his deep hatred for the man. They had crossed swords many times in the past, there was no love lost between them.

"I must congratulate you on turning up that broken cup with McMahon's fingerprints on it. As you know we've been hunting him for years. As I recall the victim and her husband were good friends of yours," remarked the chief superintendent in a flat voice, devoid of warmth or compassion.

"They still are," replied Alaister through gritted teeth.

"They still are, sir!" snapped Quinn.

"Gentlemen, if we're going to play the schoolboy, headmaster game I'm leaving. Something tells me I'm not here for a pat on the back and a *well done old chap* speech."

"Don't be so bloody insolent, McMaster."

"It's Constable McMaster to you, Quinn."

"Okay, that's enough you two!" shouted Chief Superintendent Robertson. "Alaister, you are a well-respected member of this Service, the last thing I want to do in the eleventh hour of your career is to be forced to charge you with another insubordination. You're right, this isn't about a pat on the back as you call it. The reason I've asked to see you is to inform you that the detectives in CID don't believe for one minute, your cock-and-bull story about where you found that broken cup!"

"You're looking at some serious criminal charges, McMaster, let alone Police Act charges if you stick to this lie. Your best bet is to come clean," snapped DI Quinn.

A long silence followed. Both senior officers waited in anticipation for the seasoned officer to tell them the truth, anxious to hear every word.

"The truth is, gentlemen, I was in the senior officers' berthing pen taking a dump the other day and there before my eyes was the broken cup floating in the reflection of DI Quinn at the bottom of the toilet bowl."

The detective inspector jumped to his feet, his composure gone, red faced and ready to launch an assault on the constable.

"I'm done here, unless the detective inspector wants to see me behind the bicycle sheds after school." He turned his back on the two senior officers and strode proudly out of the room.

"Thanks a lot for your invaluable assistance, Inspector!" shouted the infuriated chief superintendent.

"Well, aren't you going to suspend him, sir? That was outrageous."

"I'll deal with him later. There are other things going on at the moment of far more concern than his attitude towards management and your attitude towards the lower ranks. That will be all, Inspector. I said, that will be all, Inspector!"

Inspector Quinn skulked out of the office, unaware that under the current regime he was not being considered for promotion, for a number of reasons, his narcissism being one of them.

Constable McMaster had already lied to the detectives about where he'd found the broken piece of china with McMahon's fingerprints on it. The last thing he wanted was them descending on Harry, who, for whatever reason had been under an immense amount of stress.

Alaister decided that he'd fit the pieces of the puzzle together himself until a picture emerged that he could do something with, then he'd think about coming clean with the chief superintendent. He quite liked Robertson and he knew Robertson liked and respected him. They'd be mad at him, as it was the CID and SOCO were searching a roadside dumping ground where losers dumped old washing machines, couches and old tires on a quiet country road miles away from where Harry lived. They were going to be pissed when they learned the truth. Alaister was almost glad he was retiring in August. The one decent thing he'd done, so he thought, was to tell Erin Scott to take some annual leave. He told her that if she got roped into the search she'd end up being mad at him if the truth ever leaked out.

"Alaister McMaster; always the mysterious one," she had said. "Thanks for the heads-up. Come to think of it, I do have a sick relative in Scotland that needs my close attention. Call me when it's safe to return, Officer."

"I will, Erin. Have a safe trip. I think Jen and I should join you."

"I think the two of you should."

Chapter Seven

Storrington Police Office was more of a brick box next to a row of police houses, with the police vehicle garages behind and the tiniest vegetable plot fit for *The Guinness Book of Records* between the station and the garages, lovingly tended by one of Alaister's colleagues. The station was conveniently located just off the main street. Alaister sat at the station desk checking computer records for stolen red pick-up trucks, narrowing his field of search to Sussex and for a time frame covering the past six months. There were a few matches, but the one that caught his eye was a red Ford pick-up 4x4 found burnt-out up by Devils Dyke. He printed out the report and read it, frustrated by the lack of detail in it. *Another crappy report prepared by a lazy, disinterested police officer*, he said to himself.

He looked at the officer's name on the report. "Constable Wainwright, I should have known," he said contemptuously. "How many speeding tickets did you hand out this month, you arsehole? I bet you're still number one in the Sussex Police for sticking it to the public, but useless when it comes to doing any real police work." He was still speaking aloud when two of his colleagues entered the office having overheard him.

Constable Nick Frazer from the nearby Washington single man detachment turned to Alaister, "Didn't you hear, Alaister, they promoted that wanker last week; it's Sergeant Wainright now. Just goes to show the importance of speeding tickets to one's career."

"You've got to be bloody joking, mate! Job's f.....," said Alaister angrily.

"Job's f.....," repeated his two colleagues in agreement as they made their way out through the back door. Both men were full of respect and admiration for Constable Alaister McMaster, a man they were glad to have at their side in a tough situation.

* * *

Alaister sat staring at the printout in his hands and decided to take a drive up to Devils Dyke himself. At one time he had been a member of the Regional Crime Squad and was well respected as a hardnosed detective. Telling Detective Inspector Quinn that, *he was the worst supervisor he'd ever met and he would never work for him again,* had not been a good career move. Within twenty-four hours he was back in uniform and his career had come to a halt.

Alaister's colleagues constantly reminded him that whatever had gone wrong in his career at the hands of others with little vision, he could still wake up every morning and proudly look himself in the mirror. All that really mattered was that his wife and three grownup children still loved him and his peers respected him. What more could a man want. Alaister kept telling himself this, trying to make himself feel better, but inside he was angry and at times bitter as he saw other officers either promoted or transferred to specialist plainclothes positions.

Returning to reality, Alaister shouted through to his sergeant's office. "Sarge, I'm heading over to Devils Dyke on an enquiry this afternoon. We've got enough guys on to cover for me."

"Do I need to know the details or is this another one of those Constable McMaster investigations that I'm better off having no knowledge of?" replied Sergeant Mike Harris. "You recall what I told you when you first came to Storrington?"

"I do, Mike. You told me you'd heard I got results, you didn't want to know how I got them, but when it all went wrong, you were not going to cover for me, I was on my own."

"Precisely, Officer. You'd do well to remember that. And take heed of something else."

"And what's that, Sergeant?"

Sergeant Harris put down the papers he was reading, got up from his desk and stood in the doorway looking over the rim of his spectacles at Alaister.

"You are not retired yet, and even when you have retired, they can still come after you.

You are not bringing me down with you. I have not forgotten your last escapade; I refer to your front page newspaper article in *The West Sussex County Times* that almost caused me to have a heart attack in my local newsagent's. I quote, *police officer says lenient sentences metered out by judges and magistrates are putting police officers' lives at risk.* You were lucky not to have been suspended. Much as I respect your success and clearance rates, I shall be glad to see the back of you; the stress of being your immediate supervisor is not worth the detrimental health risks you are causing me. Alaister, you are a supervisors' nightmare."

Sergeant Harris could no longer keep the serious pretence going and a broad smiled crept across his face. "Try not to incur any overtime, Alaister, if you can help it. Unlike criminals, the Sussex Police is operating on a tight budget."

"No problem, Mike, and thanks, I shouldn't be too long. I might drop down to Brighton Police Station afterwards; you know, my old nick."

"That's fine, Alaister. By-the-way, don't forget to give me the time and venue of your leaving do; myself and Chief Superintendent Robertson want to attend, just to make sure you have actually retired you understand. Oh, and watch your speed, our brothers in the Traffic Unit have been giving out tickets to police officers in marked cars who are speeding and not on an emergency response call."

"Job's f.....," said Alaister as he walked out the door.

"Job's f.....," said Sergeant Mike Harris in agreement.

* * *

Unknowingly Alaister had driven the same route as Harry had done, through Edburton and Fulking, past his favorite pub, *the Shepherd and Dog*, and eventually on to Devils Dyke and to the track that led down to where the pick-up truck had been torched.

Alaister had to leave his police car on the road because the track was a muddy quagmire and make the rest of the way in on foot to the spot where the pick-up truck had been burnt out. It was heavy going through thick mud and he cursed himself repeatedly for not having the good sense to throw a pair of old wellies into the boot of the police car.

Eventually he arrived at the spot where it looked like the most recent act of vandalism had taken place, guessing it to be the exact spot because of the tow truck tire impressions in the mud and the burnt debris lying around on the ground in an almost circular pattern. This he reckoned was where the 4x4 had been torched.

Alaister stood looking down at the town of Brighton far off in the distance, with the English Channel in the background. His mind began to wander in the silence and desolation of this remote place. He found himself reminiscing about the many years he had been a policeman in Brighton. The good, the bad and the ugly memories flooded his mind as he cast his eyes southward towards the distant horizon. He thought about the night the IRA blew up the Grand Hotel on Brighton's seafront. The courage of *the Iron Lady*, Mrs. Thatcher, Prime Minister at the time, who despite being in the hotel when the bomb went off, narrowly cheating death herself, stood on the podium the same day and gave a rousing speech to politicians at the Brighton Conservative Party Conference.

Alaister had been on uniform patrol that night. When Mrs. Thatcher walked past him under heavy escort, he was shocked at how tiny she was, and yet how powerful. He turned his thoughts to Harry Davidson, to that night in the Brighton Lanes when Harry had saved his life, but he knew justice, wherever it lay, had to be done, no matter how bitter the taste might be. After all, he reminded himself, it was his job to uphold the law.

The pick-up truck had since been towed away to a storage pound, where it would remain until the insurance company had seen it. Alaister stood in the very spot where the truck had been. As he stood there he could feel Harry Davidson's presence. He felt it all around him. *Harry was here. I know it; I can feel it in my bones.*

Alaister felt very uncomfortable, he felt as though ghosts were swirling around him, that he was being watched by something or someone he couldn't see, something that was still in the very atmosphere that was cocooned in this piece of windswept land. He tried to imagine what he would have done if he had been Harry. *It was Harry, it had to be Harry. My gut instinct is screaming at me; that very day when I looked into Harry's eyes, that something was not quite right with this picture feeling I got. Seldom have I been wrong in my long career. On the few occasions when I have been wrong, my gut feeling was never as strong as it is now.* With the wind and a few seagulls for company, Alaister suddenly broke his own silence ...

"A taxi! That's it. Harry got a taxi that night, I know it! He wouldn't have risked anyone helping him, he's old school. But why? What the hell happened back at Rose Cottage? McMahon was inside that cottage, that's a given. Something heavy was dragged across the grass to the garage. I should have checked it. I should have gone with my instincts. Harry, you cunning old dog, you burnt the truck out; I know you did, but why? And what happened to McMahon? Probably English was with him too. They didn't burn inside the truck. You and me, Harry, are going to have another chat, after I find out which taxi firm you used and the driver who took you to wherever you went."

He trudged back through the mud to his marked police car and drove fast all the way down to Brighton Police Station to make a few phone calls and reacquaint himself with old friends.

Alaister parked the police car on John Street, right out front of Brighton Police Station on double-yellow lines. It took him a while to get to the uniform officers' parade room. It was to the left of the front entrance, at the end of a long corridor, but en route he was stopped and slapped on the back, his hand shaken vigorously by former colleagues, eager to catch-up on the latest news. A group of officers he had worked with stopped him.

"Read your article in the paper, Alaister," one of them said. "I bet the Brass liked that." Their conversation ended with the words, *Job's f......*

Finally, Alaister was alone in the parade room, apart from two young officers that looked like they were both just out of high school and didn't even look as though they had started shaving. They looked at Alaister with an air of superiority and contempt that an officer of his age was still just a constable. They didn't even reply to Alaister's, *How's it going?* Ignoring them, Alaister got on with the business in hand and began making phone calls.

It didn't take him long to hit pay dirt. Yes, one of the taxi companies, Brighton Taxis, had got a call to pick-up an Irish gentleman in the early hours of the morning, somewhere on Dyke Road Avenue, the same morning the pick-up truck was torched up at Devils Dyke. The driver,

Rob, was out on the road at the moment, but they'd get him to call the officer A.S.A.P.

"Did the man leave a name?" Alaister asked. The dispatcher thumbed through her records in between answering drivers' queries over the radio.

"Yes, he did, Seamus O'Rourke."

Half an hour later, Rob, the taxi driver called the station and spoke with Alaister. As an experienced police officer, Alaister knew the importance of writing down as much information as he could suck out of his witnesses. He wrote down all the details of Rob Winters, full name, date of birth, address and phone number. He even had him read out his driver's license number. Alaister took him back to the early morning that he was particularly interested in. He became aware of the two young upstart officers staring at him across the parade room. They were now paying close attention to him, as though realizing for the first time that a master investigator was in their midst; probably another detective returned to the uniform branch as a penance, having fallen from grace.

Rob said, "Yeah, I remember him. Nice old guy, Irish accent, said he was from Limerick. Had a small backpack with him. Picked him up at the top end of Dyke Road Avenue by Hill Top, about one in the morning. He was one tough old guy, stocky too, wouldn't have wanted to go a round with him I can tell you."

Harry Davidson, Alaister immediately thought. "Where'd he ask you to take him?"

"He told me to drop him off between Steyning and Washington on the A283. I dropped him off just west of the turn-off that leads through Ashurst to Partridge Green. I didn't feel comfortable about doing it, him being old an' all."

"Why there?"

"I dunno, he said something about a road crew picking him up there that morning."

"What else did you talk about?"

"Nothing much. I remember he was tired and wanted to take a kip, *a wee nap* was how he put it."

"What else?"

"I told him my wife was from Dublin, he said he hadn't been back since *The Troubles.* Anyway, why are you so interested in this old guy? Don't tell me he's a member of the IRA?"

"Just following up loose ends. We think he's a runaway from an old people's home, nothing more than that." The taxi driver laughed, but was unconvinced.

"How did he pay you?"

"Cash, not a bad tip either, not over the top, but generous all the same."

"Mm. Probably a stupid question. You don't happen to have any of that money do you?" The officer was almost embarrassed asking the question, but from experience he knew that, sometimes the most ridiculous question can lead to a break in a case.

"Are you kidding?"

"Pity, just a thought. I know this sounds crazy, but I want you to sit back, close your eyes and relax. Can you do that?"

"Sounds nuts to me, but sure. You're for real aren't you?"

"I'm for real. Okay, think back to that taxi ride. You're pulling up beside the curb, he's standing there, waiting for you. What's he wearing?"

Rob, somewhat embarrassed, sat back in his chair, made himself as comfortable as he could and closed his eyes, humoring the police officer.

"He's in dark clothing, jacket and pants. The collar is pulled up high and he's got a cloth cap on, it's pulled down low over his eyes, I can't see his face. Got an old backpack with him too, like from an army surplus store, dark green canvas."

"Okay, good, so he's getting into the taxi now. Think about other senses apart from sight and sound, think about smells."

"Yeah, I remember now. He smelled of petrol, not overpowering, but every so often I got a whiff of it."

"What else?" Alaister was beginning to get excited.

"Nothing really, except for the Irish accent. It's funny, I thought about that afterwards. It sounded like it was put on, I can't be sure. Being married to an Irish lass I've heard many Irish accents from mixing with all her family. Never heard one like his though, even if he is from Limerick. The best way I can describe it is like an Englishman trying to be an Irishman, God forbid."

"That's very good, Rob. What else?"

"That's it, mate. If I think of anything else I'll give you a call."

"I'd appreciate that. Listen, in case you can't get hold of me, here's my cell phone number."

Alaister knew how important it was in a serious case for witnesses to be able to get hold of the lead investigator promptly. If it was made difficult for them, they just wouldn't bother and that nugget of information they were going to give you was gone and might never come back. He thanked the taxi driver for his help and sat in silence for a few minutes before leaving the room. He didn't bother to address the two younger officers as he left. After the bustle of downtown Brighton, Alaister looked forward to driving the country roads back to *his* village.

At this point Alaister wasn't going to take a statement from Rob. He was still on a *fishing expedition*. For the first time in his whole career and for reasons he couldn't explain, nothing of this *fishing expedition* was going into his official police pocketbook, though he had made a note of everything Rob Winters had told him in a small notebook he kept with him, information he didn't want the defense lawyers knowing about. He already knew that his *box time* in the witness stand would be heavy duty; he just hoped he could dance around it and articulate the reason for the gaps in his pocketbook.

As far as he was concerned and like the majority of his colleagues, the defense lawyers of today weren't interested in justice, they were more interested in prestige, money, power, glamour, just like the new breed of television celebrities. He had a lot of respect for the older ones he'd come up against. The courtroom battles were always dirty, but afterwards it was business as usual. There were the chosen few that he shook hands with after a grueling court case, even though they had given him a whipping on the stand. Sometimes they would meet later for lunch and a beer. Others he had come across he loathed and resented everything they stood for. They and the crappy justice system were one of the reasons he so looked forward to retirement, along with the ineffective police leadership; men and women who had long since lost the reality of policing the streets. They had forgotten their roots, sold their souls to get ahead. If that was what promotion was all about, Alaister McMaster never wanted to be a part of it. Many had become full of their own importance. He thought of them as peacocks, strutting around like little tin gods. Halfway home his cell phone rang.

"Hello."

"Constable McMaster?"

"Yeah, who's this?"

"It's Rob Winters, the taxi driver."

"Oh, right, sorry, mate. Hang on let me pull off the road." Alaister stopped his police car by an open gate leading into a hay field. He reversed into the gap that allowed a tractor to gain access to the field. "What can I do for you?"

"I forgot all about it. That old guy, he gave me a five pound note for a tip."

"What of it?"

"I remembered after I spoke to you. I gave it to my son for pocket money. I checked, he's still got it in his bedroom at home."

"Is anyone home now?"

"Yeah, my wife will be there. My son's gone for soccer practice, says he wants to play for Manchester United one day."

"Good team. Tell your wife I'll be there in half an hour. Tell her not to let anyone else touch that note, I'll put it in an evidence bag myself when I get there. Don't worry I'll replace the note with another one. Oh, and Rob."

"Yeah."

"Thanks, mate."

Alaister accelerated quickly out of his parking spot, the traffic was busy and a gap had just opened up. The tires of his police car spun on the loose gravel before making the tarmac road, he floored the accelerator and headed back into town, down to the sprawling council house development called Moulscoomb, a tough neighborhood affectionately known by the Brighton coppers as, *The Scum*. But for those who had worked that area there were still many good, honest and hardworking folk living amongst the criminal element that seemed to migrate to this spawning ground of undesirables.

Mrs. Winters, a hardnosed woman in her mid-thirties answered the door. She had the ubiquitous permed hair that seemed a must for the neighborhood. She carried the spare tire of a woman whose last serious attempt at exercise was back in primary school, a diet of junk food had done the rest. The house was clean, that was a change, thought Alaister. At least he didn't have to wipe his feet when leaving the house.

There were so many houses he had been in that stunk of soiled nappies, rotting garbage, dog shit, cat shit, body odor and engine oil. Many a time, especially in the height of the summer he had to conduct an inquiry outside on the front garden instead of inside the house. He would begin to gag, turn and walk outside, holding his breath and stifling the urge to vomit. In the beginning he was polite about it, the older and more jaded he became the more blunt he was, telling the occupants, *Christ, your house stinks, I can't talk to you in here*. They would follow him outside telling him they were sorry for the mess, they hadn't done any housework that day. Alaister would shake his head in exasperation, aware that it would take a squadron from the army a week to clean-up the house. The stench of filth ingrained into their clothing, the foul smell seeping out as he spoke to them, doing his best to keep his distance. When he got back into his own police car the smell had ingrained itself into his own clothing. He always felt sorry for the children living under such disgusting conditions. Alaister would sarcastically joke to his colleagues that, *Third World poverty is on our own doorstep*, only he wasn't joking, he was being deadly serious.

Alaister followed Mrs. Winters' stocky frame and large backside up to her son's bedroom. A poster of the Manchester United football team at their home ground at Old Trafford hung proudly above his bed. His bedspread and pillowcase were the same colors as the Manchester United football team, red and white. *A real boy's room*, thought Alaister. Mrs. Winters opened the top drawer of her son's dresser and brought out a small, black metal moneybox with gold painted edging. She handed it begrudgingly to Alaister. From the look on her face he thought she was expecting him to immediately run out of the house with it tucked under his arm.

"It's in there and mind you replace it," she snapped.

Alaister opened the box and using his pen, carefully lifted out the only five pound note in the box and placed it into a brown paper evidence bag. He then, more out of anger at her remark, took out a ten pound note from his own wallet and put it back in the boy's moneybox. He made sure Mrs. Winters saw what he had done. He looked her straight in the eyes, his anger quite apparent.

"Your boy seems like he's a good kid, you make sure he keeps the extra five pounds courtesy of the Sussex Police, namely me."

He left the house feeling annoyed. He was mad at himself because he could scarcely afford to spare five pounds of his own money, let alone ten. That money was for his extra treats when working, now he was going to have to go without until payday.

By the time he got back to the village police station in Storrington, after a pleasant drive across the South Downs, Mrs. Winters was forgotten, as was the loss of his money. He did think however, as he was driving back, that if he was given one wish at that moment it would be that the young Winters boy got to play for Manchester United one day.

Back at the police station, Alaister McMaster telephoned Scenes of Crimes and asked to speak with Erin Scott.

"That really was good work on your part, Alaister, that print has caused quite a stir, as you already know. Hopefully it will prove a useful lead to catching that bastard McMahon and his sidekick English. The office is buzzing with excitement. I'll give you the heads-up though. I have been instructed by the Brass to report any conversations I have with you, and if asked to do any SOCO work for you in the future, I am to seize whatever it is you want examined and to call them straightaway."

"The good work was done by you too, Erin. I know some Scenes of Crimes officers that would have told me I was wasting my time and would have said, *You won't get anything on this*."

"Now, now, Constable McMaster, that's not very nice."

"I suppose then you won't be interested in doing a chemical test on a five pound note I've got. It'd be nice to put another piece of the puzzle into the jigsaw."

"I'm busy at the moment." Erin immediately hung-up the phone and quickly walked out of the office. When she felt it was safe she called Alaister on his cell phone.

"McMaster."

"Alaister, are you trying to get me suspended!"

"Of course not, Erin," replied Alaister, taken aback by her abrupt remark. "Okay, okay, I'll get someone else to do it."

"It's not that, Alaister, they know you're up to something. I suppose you've heard the rumors going around about you?"

"Rumors, what rumors, what are you talking about, Erin?"

"Okay, it's just what I've been overhearing. The rumor is that you've tracked down the two rapists, or one of them at least, that raped Melissa Markham."

Alaister interrupted her. "I'd hardly call it rape, Erin, they practically killed her," he snapped back.

"I'm sorry, I didn't mean to make it sound like that, I know it was brutal, you forget, I helped work on the case. Not only that, Melissa and I were very good friends, still are very good friends."

"I'm sorry, Erin, I didn't mean to …" she cut him off.

"They say you've either killed them and buried their bodies or you're planning to and that's why the Brass are watching you. I wouldn't be surprised if they've stuck surveillance on you and have your phone bugged as well as a tracking device on your personal car. All I'm saying is, you need to watch your back. As for me, I don't care, in fact I hope they're dead, they both deserve to die anyway. Look, let's meet for coffee, our usual place and be mindful of a tail. I'll see what I can do to help you without me landing in shit."

"Okay, I'm just about done here. I'll meet you there in, say, an hour."

"See you there in an hour, and remember what I said about surveillance." Before Alaister could reply, Erin hung up on him.

Alaister decided not to use his police car and not incur any overtime. There would be too many awkward questions. He phoned Jen and left a message on her cell phone. His wife was still working at the hospital and wouldn't be home for a few more hours anyway.

It took Alaister ages to find a parking spot near Brighton seafront, having driven round and round the block with increasing frustration. Finally, one became available on Grand Parade, only a short walk to the bus station at Pool Valley. He did not go straight to the rendezvous point but made a point of walking in the opposite direction of where he wanted to go. He circled the same street twice, sometimes three times, then ducked into Hanningtons, the huge department store on North Street, ducked out through a rear door and walked quickly towards the seafront. Finally, convinced he was not being followed he walked into the Mock Turtle Café in Pool Valley. Erin was already sitting at a table in the corner.

"I've ordered coffee for you and your favorite éclair," she said as Alaister sat down opposite her. "My treat, you paid last time," she smiled. "Now tell me what you've got."

"You're not wearing a wire are you, Erin?" Alaister looked at her for any sign of betrayal.

"Don't be so bloody stupid. It's me, Alaister. You know what; sod you!" She got up tears in her eyes; Alaister grabbed her wrist before she could leave.

"I'm sorry, Erin, I was out of order, that was totally uncalled for."

"Alaister, I'm your friend. Always have been always will be; no matter what." She took a tissue from her handbag as she sat back down and dabbed her eyes. "What are you staring at now, Alaister McMaster?"

"How beautiful you are, Erin," he smiled.

"Oh, please, enough. What have you got?"

"I've got a fiver in my pocket, it's another one of my long shots. I'd like you to see if you can find any interesting prints on it and, if you do, let me know before you speak to anyone else. If you can't get hold of me call me on my cell."

"Okay, hand it over, I'm going to record it officially, do everything by the book except I'll have amnesia regarding notifying Professional Standards. You're on their trail aren't you, Alaister? I hope you find them. Don't worry, after you've buried them I'll still come and visit you in prison." Alaister gave her the incident number again, relating to the burnt-out Ford pick-up truck. "Listen, Alaister, if I find anything you better have a damn good story."

"I'll think of something. How soon can you do this?"

"As soon as I get back to the lab I'll start working on it. I'll call you if I find any prints. It'll be your call if you want me to submit them to NAFIS."

"If you find any that are suitable to submit, go ahead and submit them."

"Alaister, you know there'll be a shit-storm if your suspects' names match any prints I find. Look, I don't even want to know where you got that five pound note, the less I know the less I can tell them when they start torturing me. Suspended on full pay. Mm, that doesn't sound so bad."

The two of them got up and embraced. Alaister was surprised when Erin kissed him on the lips. He could feel himself blushing as the tall, attractive leggy brunette sashayed her way out of the café, glancing once over her shoulder, with a saucy smile.

* * *

It was a boring Wednesday afternoon, five weeks had passed since Alaister last spoke to Erin. His cell phone rang.

"Hi, Alaister, it's Erin. You won't believe it when I tell you!"

"Don't tell me McMahon's fingerprints are on that note."

"No, even better. I found a couple of others that didn't match anyone on the system, but Justin English's prints are on it. Who's a clever boy? I can see you getting an instant promotion."

"I don't think so, Erin. I need a couple of days to follow-up a lead I'm working on. I know this is asking a lot, but please keep this under your hat. Can you give me till noon Friday?"

"Chief Superintendent Gray isn't going to like this, Alaister. It's already leaked out; the NAFIS girl opened her big mouth. You don't have until Friday, you don't even have until today. The Team they've got working on this case is going to ask for your head on a platter. That prick DCI Knight in Professional Standards called me up to his office; I had to use my *ace-in-the-hole* to save myself."

"What happened?"

"He started off about how I was going to find myself suspended and getting four years for conspiracy, obstruction and so on. I reminded him of the time he put his hand up my skirt at the Christmas party and how that information becoming public knowledge wouldn't be good for his career."

"You never told me any of this, Erin."

"It was on a need to know basis, Alaister, one of those things I keep in my little black book for a rainy day. Anyway, I don't tell you everything, and you certainly don't tell me everything that's bloody obvious," she said sounding annoyed.

"Touché. So what was his reaction when you kicked him in the nuts, metaphorically speaking that is? "

"He went bright red, shook with rage for a moment and finally asked me to leave his office; well, he didn't actually ask me to leave, his actual words were, *Get the f out of my office!*' I said, *With respect, sir, I presume we have an understanding?* He nodded in agreement, I gave him my best sexy smile and left."

"Erin, I'm so sorry, are you okay?"

"I'm fine, but you can expect to be summoned to *the Ivory Tower*, and no doubt his frustration will be taken out on you. He's gunning for you big time, Alaister. If I were you I'd put your papers in today and retire. You're going to be retiring in a few months anyway, August isn't it?"

"That's right and make sure you're there for the grand farewell."

"Of course I'll be there. Just remember after you've gone, that's if they haven't suspended you or locked you up, I am still going to be working for a living. And another thing, which you keep forgetting, the Markhams are my friends too. I want those bastards caught just as much as you do. What they did to poor Melissa was despicable. Be careful, Alaister, I'm not so sure that taking the law into your own hands is really the right way to deal with this. Do I make myself clear?"

"Who says I'm taking the law into my own hands?"

"Alaister, it's me Erin. Did you forget who you were talking to? I know you." Alaister didn't reply. "Are you listening to me?"

"Loud and clear, Erin."

"Okay then; good luck. You better have a good story about where you got that five pound note from and remember; they're watching you,

Alaister." Click went the phone again before Alaister could reply. Erin was not one for long telephone conversations.

Alaister reflected for a moment on how good a friend Erin was. She was one of only a handful of truly solid friends he trusted, one he could entrust his own life with. The reflective moment wàs broken by his police radio squawking. *November Two Zero Nine report to the chief superintendent's office Horsham Police Station.* Having acknowledged the dispatcher, Alaister turned his police car around and began heading reluctantly towards Horsham, a feeling of doom beginning to descend over him. Always conscious of officer safety, Alaister called up Sergeant Mike Harris to let him know they were going to be a man down and the reason why.

On the way to Horsham Police Station, Alaister decided that the best way to deflect the problem about the five pound note was to be as truthful as possible. He wasn't going to tell the whole truth; but to lie, he had learned over the years was a recipe for disaster. You never knew exactly how much *they* knew. You didn't want to give away too much, you just had to feel them out. It was well known that police officers when under investigation were useless at keeping quiet and most of the time they folded like a cardboard box left out in the rain. But not Constable Alaister McMaster, he was too wily for that, and the Brass knew it. It was often said that Constable McMaster would have made a really successful criminal had he not become a police officer. Only Harry Davidson knew the real truth about the five pound note and Alaister wasn't about to leak that information just yet.

* * *

Alaister sat in the hallway outside Chief Superintendent Bernie Robertson's office. He knew he would be left sitting out there to stew, but at his age and length of service he didn't stew anymore. He normally sat back, closed his eyes and went to sleep. Inevitably when the Brass came out to get him they were the ones that became stressed, not Alaister, especially when they had to wake him up.

Twenty minutes later the door opened and Detective Inspector Quinn, newly appointed to the Professional Standards Branch, emerged from Chief Superintendent Robertson's office, a malicious grin across his face. Alaister sensed his unpleasant presence and opened his eyes.

"Hemorrhoids troubling you again, Inspector?"

"Very funny, McMaster. Your smile will soon be wiped off your face after Detective Chief Inspector Knight from Professional Standards has finished with you."

Alaister followed his nemeses into the office. Detective Chief Inspector Knight was seated behind Chief Superintendent Robertson's desk, scowling up at him.

"Inspector, I think the DCI's got the same problem as you," remarked Alaister on seeing the detective chief inspector's sour face."

The DCI didn't rise to the bait. Alaister wasn't about to remain standing on the other side of the large desk like a naughty little schoolboy either. He sat down in one of the two remaining chairs and made himself comfortable.

"Well, what's all this about then, sir, someone been stealing the chief constable's underpants off the washing line?" Inspector Quinn was bristling with rage.

"You, McMaster, are treading a very thin tightrope, a very thin tightrope indeed. Don't think for one minute this will all go away when you've retired. I will make it my business to see you charged criminally, so you can forget about holidaying in Majorca, or wherever the hell you intend on going when you retire. Your view won't be of the blue ocean, coconut palms and girls in grass skirts, but one of four walls in a prison cell. Do I make myself clear! What are you fiddling with man?"

"I'm sorry, sir, my tape recorder got stuck in my pocket. I just wanted to let you know I was going to tape our little meeting. Now, what was that again, something about charging me criminally. If that's where we're going with this, gentlemen, number one, a caution from you would be a good idea, Judges Rules and all. No offence, gentlemen."

"If at this stage I thought that was going to be necessary, Constable, I'd be talking to you down in the cells. Where did you get that five pound note from with English's fingerprints on it!" shouted the DCI, red faced and eyes bulging with anger.

"Why didn't you ask me that in the first place? It's really quite simple." He looked up at DI Quinn, hovering over him. The DI looked as though he was struggling with strong inner emotions that were telling him to strangle Alaister and those emotions were beginning to get the better of him. Always the bully when it came to dealing with the lower ranks, Quinn wasn't used to a constable not being intimidated by him. Alaister added fuel to the fire.

"Detective Inspector Quinn, sit down there's a good fellow, you're making the place look untidy." DI Quinn grabbed the chair next to Alaister and sat down, immediately regretting doing so the moment his large backside met the seat. Alaister continued, "Now I'll tell you both a story about being a simple beat copper ..."

Alaister explained to the two men how he had been going through the police bulletins at the Storrington police office when he came across the information about the burnt-out Ford pick-up truck at Devils Dyke. He'd seen a similar truck nosing around the village about the time they'd had a spree of burglaries. On a whim he decided to look into it further. He told them about the taxi driver and how he came across the five pound note. The way he described it, to an outsider it all sounded like good old fashioned policing, but to Knight and Quinn it sounded like some very good police work mixed with a private agenda and a lot of smoke and mirrors. Alaister never mentioned Erin's SOCO work and the DCI never once brought it up.

"Let me give you some advice, McMaster." Alaister didn't bother to correct DCI Knight on his title of constable, things so far were going well for him and he didn't want to spoil it. "If you track down McMahon and English you will, I repeat, you will, notify me immediately, do you understand?"

"Yes sir, absolutely, sir."

"And if I am not available, anyone in upper Command. Do I make myself clear? If you do not I will see to it personally that you are arrested at the very least for obstruction of justice!"

"Yes sir."

"One other thing. I had the serial number on that bank note run through the data bank ..."

"That was going to be my next move," interrupted Alaister.

"Well, I'll have saved you the time, won't I," said DCI Knight sarcastically. He picked up some papers from his desk. "Last autumn there was an armed robbery at a Nat West bank in Croydon. A young female cashier was shot and seriously injured, to my knowledge, she's still in a wheelchair. That fiver you recovered was part of the bait money stolen from the bank. Don't play the bloody hero, McMaster. DI Quinn and I want those two men just as much as you do."

"Of course you do, sir. It would do wonders for your careers I'm sure," replied Alaister insolently.

"Get out!" shouted the DCI. Alaister didn't bother to respond, he got up and left the room abruptly. "David, is the surveillance team still in play?"

"Yes sir, they are. Shall I give the word on the new operation, sir?"

"I just did," replied Detective Chief Inspector Knight.

Quinn picked up the phone on the desk and made a call. When he replaced the receiver after briefly speaking to the DI in charge of the Sussex Police Surveillance Unit, known as *The Commandos*, he turned to his boss and said, "Operation Magnet is live, sir."

"Good, very good. Keep me updated, Inspector. It'll only be a matter of time before we have him this time."

"What do you want me to do about Ms. Scott, our SOCO officer, sir?" The DCI looked up unnecessarily embarrassed, which surprised the inspector.

"Nothing, I've already spoken to her and she's been warned off. We'll see how things play out with our target McMaster. If he contacts her again we'll review the situation once more concerning her."

* * *

At eleven o'clock Thursday morning, Alaister McMaster entered the long, winding laneway that led up to Rose Cottage. He knew that, generally speaking, Harry would be back from his walk with the dogs. Kingsley, the ruddy-faced gamekeeper stepped in front of the police car and raised his palm for the officer to stop. Nestled under his right arm he carried a double-barreled shotgun. Kingsley was a short, stocky man with a barrel chest dressed in his usual green tweed jacket and matching cap, brown corduroy trousers, green wellington boots and to complete his haute couture, his jacket was tied around the middle with a piece of baler twine, not orange polypropylene, but sisal. He reminded Alaister of a revolutionary guard at some eastern bloc border control checkpoint about to demand, *Papers*. His beautiful black Labrador retriever, Bess stood obediently by his side. Alaister watched the man approach, thinking to himself, *Kingsley would have made a great police officer and a damn good sergeant.* The gamekeeper walked up to the driver's door as Alaister drew up alongside him and wound down the window.

"You won't get up there in that, Alaister, mud's far too deep," said Kingsley in his strong Sussex accent.

"Good morning, Kingsley. Thank you for telling me. How's the poaching business these days?"

"Chased a couple off last night as a matter of fact. Out there lampin' they were. If you get a report of someone with an arse full of bird shot, mum's the word right?"

"Absolutely, Kingsley. If another police officer comes to see you, remember the drill?"

"Act concerned, look surprised and deny, deny, deny," smiled Kingsley.

"Good man, Kingsley, I've got you well trained."

"You've always been fair with me, Alaister, can't deny you that. I 'ear you're leaving the Force in the summer, that'll be a sad day for this village."

"That's kind of you to say so, Kingsley, mind you there's a few around here that will be glad to see the back of me."

"That's because they're crooks, Alaister. I reckon they'll have more to fear from you being retired than in uniform, they'd be pretty stupid to bad mouth you when you're back in civvy street. Anyway, you goin' up to see old 'arry, cos if you are I'll give you a ride up in the Land Rover and if you're not likely to be too long I'll wait for you in the lane. I don't mind doin' that, the view's gorgeous from up there."

"Kingsley, you're a diamond."

"Right you are then, pull that excuse for a vehicle off the lane and park it by the side there. I hope you don't mind Bess comin' for the ride?"

"Not at all."

They slipped and slid their way along the lane, even in four-wheel drive it was a tricky journey.

"It's good of you to keep an eye on the old boy, Alaister, 'e 'ad quite the fall just before Christmas they tell me. Well, I haven't seen you to talk to since way before Christmas mind you."

"That reminds me, thanks for the brace of pheasants, that was very thoughtful of you."

"Well, I didn't want you out there poachin' did I? That wouldn't look very good for an officer of the law."

"How have Harry's dogs been lately, Kingsley?"

"Is this business or pleasure, Constable McMaster?"

"It's a bit of both actually; I just wanted to see how everything was."

"Sure," said Kingsley, not believing a word. "Anyway, just lately they've been a lot better. Around Christmas time you couldn'a got near 'em. I don't know what the 'ell got into 'em. Right bloody mean they were, very unlike 'em too. 'arry seems to have got 'em back to their old selves again though. It would kill 'im to have those dogs put down, they're 'is life they are. Bloody good protection too, I might add."

There was a lull in the conversation. The two men lost in their private thoughts as they bumped along the lane towards Rose Cottage. Kingsley finally broke the silence.

"You know, funny you should ask about them dogs. It would 'ave been late autumn if me memory serves me correct. Late mornin' it was, maybe twelve noon or thereabouts. I was way over t'other side of beech woods, gettin' me a few rabbits for supper I was, when I 'eard the most ferocious sound I've ever 'eard from dogs in me whole life. Now, I didn't 'ear it too well mind you, on account of the wind gettin' up as I remember, it was kind of like comin' and goin', kinda like someone turnin' a radio up and then down, then up again, if you get my meanin'. You know, fadin' in an' out like. It didn't last for too long, but I distinctly remember it made the 'airs on the back of me neck go up and me blood run cold. Made old Bess cower on the ground. Even rolled over an' peed 'erself she did, that's how bad it was."

As a good investigator, Alaister McMaster knew not to interrupt a witness when they were in full flow, if you did, they invariably lost their train of thought and the important piece of information never got told. He sat there taking it all in, the puzzle almost complete.

"Anyway," continued Kingsley. "I kept meanin' to ask 'arry about it, but never got round to it. When I did drive by one afternoon afterwards, 'e was out there with the two

Rottweilers and everythin' seemed normal and I forgot all about it, 'till you just mentioned it that is."

Kingsley pulled up in front of Rose Cottage. Alaister, dressed in his uniform slid out of the passenger seat. He felt a little uncomfortable about the dogs as he began to traipse through the mud towards the back door of the cottage.

"Ask 'im if he needs any shoppin' from the village will you!" shouted Kingsley after him. Alaister raised a hand to acknowledge he had heard. The dogs began barking aggressively inside the cottage, then he heard Harry's commanding voice.

"That'll do, you two, that'll do!"

Harry opened the door a crack, the two huge dogs had their snouts pressed one above the other into the opening, trying to pry their way out and sniffing the air to assess if the person outside was friend or foe.

"Back up, you two, let the man in. It's Constable McMaster, you know him."

The two dogs edged away from the door, their dark brown eyes fixed on the door as it was slowly swung open to reveal the man they already knew standing behind it.

"Better come in, Alaister. I'll have to reacquaint you with Jack and Jill. Something or someone must have upset them when I was away from the cottage; they're not as trusting as they used to be."

"They're just being protective, that's all."

"I see Kingsley brought you up, that was nice of him. Good man that one but bloody nosey. I suppose he's waiting for you so I presume your business won't be long. Come, my beauties, come and say hello to Alaister."

Jack and Jill stalked across the kitchen floor. It was as though they sensed the police officer was not at Rose Cottage with good tidings for their master.

The dogs tolerated Alaister stroking the tops of their huge heads, whereas before they would have been all over him, wagging their tails with excitement, but not today. Harry knew they would never again be the same dogs they had once been before the burglary. Victoria, Melanie and Michelle were the only people they had not changed their attitude towards.

"Well, sit down, Alaister. I'm sorry I was so short with you the last time you came, especially after all you've done for me."

"Forget it. How's the head, you've got quite the scar there, Harry, I see?"

"Heads fine, brains are mush though. Can I get you a tea or coffee, something stronger maybe?"

"No thanks, that's okay. Look, I want you to listen to what I've got to say Harry, or should I call you, Seamus O'Rourke."

Alaister knew that during an interrogation interview, over seventy-five percent of the suspect's communication was nonverbal. As an investigator in major crime he'd spent a lot of time studying interrogation techniques. He knew all the nonverbal cues. Harry's eyes widened just a little too much. He folded his arms across his chest and tucked his legs under his seat before replying. Alaister noticed each subtle nuance, acutely aware he was on the right track.

"What are you talking about, man?" Harry almost shouted. The dogs began a low growl and edged closer to Alaister.

"Down!" shouted Harry. Jack and Jill dropped to the floor, their eyes still fixed on Constable McMaster.

"I know two men were in your house, Harry."

"It's a cottage, not a house," interrupted Harry who was trying to compose himself, and trying hard to remember what the army had taught him almost sixty-years ago, about how to handle an interrogation. *Name, rank and number that was it.*

The officer knew Harry had a short fuse and also knew that the most important thing about an interrogation was to have the suspect like you. The minute they stopped liking you the interview was essentially over. He began to sense that Harry was beginning to stop liking him. The two dogs certainly were and Harry wasn't going to be far behind them either.

"Okay, I'll lay it out for you, Harry."

"You'll bugger off, that's what you'll do, Constable Alaister McMaster!"

The dogs were on their feet again, growling more aggressively, lips curled back, teeth bared. This time Harry did not tell them to lie down. Alaister did not want this to be confrontational. He only had a second or two before Harry literally threw him out.

"Do you remember on the news about a year ago a policeman's wife getting badly beaten and raped by two men in this county?"

"Sure I do, the f'ing bastards. It was all over the news and in the papers. Why?"

"They're good friends of mine and the two men that did that were in your bloody house, cottage or whatever the hell you want to call it!"

Harry was stunned, speechless. It was obvious his friend, Alaister McMaster, was telling the truth. He was surprised to see the police officer's eyes filled with tears.

"Go on," said Harry. "I hope you're not taping this conversation?"

"No, I'm not, Harry," replied Alaister indignantly. He undid his tunic, opened it, grabbed his shirt and tore it open, sending buttons pinging across the kitchen. "Satisfied?"

"All right, all right. Is this conversation man-to-man, off the record like or official? What I want to be certain of is this. Are you, Constable McMaster, talking to me or the Alaister McMaster I regard as a true friend and a man I respect and above all; trust?"

"Harry, I'll be straight with you. It's somewhere between the two, I won't lie to you. I've already stuck my neck out on this one. I'm the only one who knows Harry; at this point that is. To be honest I don't think the detectives will figure out what I already know because at the moment I deliberately put them off the scent, though admittedly I put them on the scent to start with. They don't have a clue that McMahon and English were here. That piece of cup that was smashed on your pathway, I had it fingerprinted. It had McMahon's prints on it. I also know you torched the stolen pick-up truck they were using, up at Devils Dyke. That five pound note you gave to the taxi driver for a tip? He gave it to his son for pocket money. Low and behold that note has English's fingerprints on it and likely yours, but seeing as you don't have a criminal record they can't match your prints on the system." He decided not to add, *Unless I get a warrant to have your fingerprints taken.*

Harry looked on dispassionately, trying hard not to give anything away, though he already knew the police officer had enough to sink him.

"The only thing I don't know yet, Harry, is what happened to McMahon and English. Just answer me one question before I leave."

"Depends on the question."

"Did you kill either of those men?"

"No, I didn't." His reply was cold and matter-of-fact.

"Do you know what happened to them?"

"That's two questions, you said only one. I think it's time you were leaving and I was calling my lawyer. Good day, Constable McMaster. I'm not answering anymore of your questions." Then Harry lost it. "Get out! Get out of my house!" He shouted so loud it woke Kingsley up, who had fallen asleep behind the wheel in the Land Rover outside.

Alaister couldn't think of anything sensible to say, he was so taken aback. "A minute ago Harry it was a cottage."

Jack and Jill were now in attack mode. Not since the fight in the Brighton Lanes years ago, when Harry had saved Alaister McMaster's life had the officer ever seen him so angry.

"I should have let them kill you that night," snarled Harry. "Instead I saved your miserable hide and this is how you repay a friend. Well, I'll tell you something, Constable McMaster, you can go to your friends, to the policeman's wife who was savagely raped and you can tell her that justice has been done. Now do your worst. Let me make arrangements for the dogs before you take me away, but I never killed anybody or had anybody killed. I just know that justice was done and that's all I'm saying and all I'll ever say to you or anyone else."

The two men eyed each other. Strong, proud men. A silence filled the cottage. A long silence. The men continued to face each other. The dogs standing quietly, appeared to sense something powerful had passed between the two men, something unspoken. Soon both men would know it too.

"Put the kettle on you miserable old bastard," smiled Alaister through his tears. *God, I love the old guy and if it hadn't been for him I wouldn't even be here now. I wouldn't even be retiring, I'd just be another forgotten police officer pushing up daisies.*

"I'll do that, Alaister. Tell busybody outside I'll run you back to your car."

Both men closed the gap between them and embraced each other, rocking one another in a bear like hug. Harry wept openly, all the stress of the past few months pouring out, but despite his moment of weakness, he resigned himself to say no more about what had taken place that fateful autumn day at Rose Cottage. Not now, not ever. That was something he would take to the grave with him. He'd deal with it when he reached the gates of heaven and had to answer to God first and then to Catherine, *or maybe it's the other way around*, he silently mused.

When Alaister returned to the cottage, after thanking a puzzled looking Kingsley for waiting, Jack and Jill were all over him like old times, pushing each other out of the way to get his affection.

"Tis a cold day out there, Officer, I have the very thing to warm the cockles of your heart." Harry shuffled over to the antique oak dresser, opened the cupboard door and lifted out a bottle of good Irish whiskey. He returned the bottle to the kitchen table and poured them both a generous glass of the elixir. "And what shall we raise our glasses to, Officer?"

"To justice having been done and strong friendship!" roared Alaister, standing to attention at the kitchen table.

"Aye. To justice having been done and strong friendship!' agreed Harry as he too stood to attention standing directly across the table from his younger friend. The two men leant forward and chinked their glasses solidly into one another's.

"Stay and have lunch with me, Alaister. Let me charge that glass of yours before we get started."

The two friends prepared a plate full of strong cheddar cheese and roast beef sandwiches with Colman's mustard. Harry prepared it from powder, to which he added two crushed cloves of fresh garlic and some horseradish sauce. The meal was washed down with copious supplies of cold Guinness.

Alaister was drunk well before Harry. Like all good drunks they never really accept their predicament, whether they are wearing a policeman's uniform or not. For some reason, that defies logic, a drunk thinks he can still drive. There was no way Harry was letting Alaister anywhere near a vehicle, let alone his police car.

While the police officer lay passed out in the armchair, his blue thermal *Marks and*

Spencer undershirt clearly visible under his ripped police shirt, Harry telephoned down to the village station.

"Is that you, Mike?"

"Harry, how are you?"

"I'm just fine, Mike, but I'm afraid Alaister isn't. Let's just say he's got a nasty headache and is not fit for duty, if you get my meaning."

The two men spoke at length. Sergeant Mike Harris was very understanding, he himself owed Harry Davidson a favor or two, but then, that's how it is in rural policing.

"Jesus Christ!" shouted Alaister, as he came-to, early in the evening. "They'll have a search party out looking for me. Quick, Harry, drive me back to my car. God knows how I'm going to explain this one."

"Your car won't be there, boy. Mike, your sergeant's picked it up. He said to tell you to have a lie in and not to bother getting in till about ten o'clock in the morning and to go home early at the end of shift. He said if you feel like shit in the morning not to bother coming in at all. He'll sign you in and out if necessary, unless the Brass asks after you. I phoned your good wife too. She says you can stay the night here and she says she loves you. I don't even think Catherine would have let me away with that one."

"You're a good man, Harry, I don't care what people say about you. You're sure my wife's not mad at me?"

"She said if you were staying the night with anyone else she'd be concerned."

"She doesn't know you very well then," chuckled Alaister.

"Very funny, McMaster. Anyway, we'll see how you fare in the morning. I think I need to eat again, I'm hungry and another Guinness would go down well too. Care to join me?"

Alaister raised his hand in salute and the two men prepared another meal like a couple of bachelors. They plonked themselves down on the couch in front of the fire in the lounge with grilled steak, baked potatoes, spinach and Guinness and watched the soccer game. Manchester United was playing Chelsea. Alaister thought about the boy in Moulscoomb. Except for one piece of the puzzle, which he always thought of as the *justice piece*, the whole puzzle was complete.

Chapter Eight

Friday afternoon all hell broke loose. Chief Superintendent Gray, a tall, balding stocky man with huge ears that stuck out at right angles, was in his office dressed immaculately in his uniform; black shoes shining like polished ebony. He was in overall charge of Professional Standards. The Brass liked a hatchet man, that was Gray. They'd sent him overseas on a secondment to Uganda, trying to teach Ugandan police officers to adopt a more British style of policing when dealing with the Ugandan population. He was a good administrator, an attribute that had helped get him promoted. Never much of a street cop, he'd had a meteoric rise through the ranks partly because of his university degree, not that biology had much to do with policing unless you were in forensics, but it had paved the way for his acceptance into the Brams Hill Staff College for accelerated promotion.

Detective Inspector Quinn had just personally briefed him on the five-pound note found by Constable McMaster. Gray was so angry he couldn't contain his rage sitting behind his desk and had to stand up and pace around his office, shouting obscenities about the constable.

"You mark my words, Detective Inspector, McMaster is dirty, do you hear me, dirty! I will make it my business to put that man behind bars for a very long time indeed, instead of retiring to prune roses in the bloody countryside!"

"Yes sir, we have him under surveillance as we speak, sir, I'm sure it will only be a matter … " Chief Superintendent Gray cut him off in mid-sentence.

"He deliberately tampered with evidence as far as I'm concerned. And as for mysteriously finding that five-pound note along with that piece of broken china, I don't buy it! He bloody well knows what's happened to McMahon and English and has had us on a search for the Holy Grail! Furthermore, he was not part of *Operation Dark Shadow* that I personally setup to find McMahon and English. He's been out there operating like some lone Dirty Harry wannabe, no doubt looking for glory! You know what I think, Inspector?"

"No, sir."

"I think McMaster has something to do with the disappearance of those two shitheads. I told you, he's dirty, put money on it. I want a surveillance team put on him twenty-four hours a day."

"They're already on him, sir, have been for a long time."

Chief Superintendent Grey ignored him as though he hadn't even heard him.

"Seven days a week and if I hear he spots them, you can rest assured the surveillance team will be back in uniform in under one hour. I want to be briefed at the end of every day, understood?"

"Yes sir, I'll see to it right away."

"Right away's too slow, I want it done yesterday!"

"Yes sir." Detective Inspector Quinn was glad to have escaped the room, loathing Constable McMaster with every breath he took. By the time he reached his own office he had begun to have heart palpitations. "That sodding McMaster is going to give me a heart attack!" he shouted. When he woke up he was in the ICU at the Royal Sussex County Hospital in Brighton.

Detective Inspector Carter took over the duties of Detective Inspector Quinn, who was recuperating in hospital, suffering from severe stress. He had suffered a heart attack. The doctors and nurses told him bluntly, that the way he was going it was only a matter of time before he had a fatal heart attack, if he didn't change his lifestyle that is. This had been a wake-up call for him. *Most people aren't so lucky to even get that*, the doctor told him somberly. *You need rest and recuperation and no stress, absolutely no stress.*

* * *

Alaister McMaster had a long memory and an unforgiving nature. Wrongs had to be righted, imbalances balanced. It was to him the *Ying and Yang* of life. He wasn't going to waste his own time balancing the books on this one, he'd do it in police time and use the police car for the long drive. He had at last taken a leaf out of his wife's book and over the years come to see the merit in her wisdom.

She would tell him, *You don't think for one minute that your bosses are at home fretting over you, give your head a shake if you think that, Alaister. Do you think they're losing any sleep over the wronged Constable McMaster. The only one that's hurting is you. I'm tired of you coming home always moaning about the wrongs of the Sussex Police and those bastards in management. Nothing's ever going to change, you can't keep fighting everyone's battles for them; you'll never win. Let the younger officers carry the load now, Alaister, enjoy your time off with me. You're letting them get to you and bringing them home into our house. It stops today; right now."*

She was right and he knew it, but there was just one last thing he had to do, he just couldn't let this one go. This one was very, very personal. The injustice had burned inside him like hot coals for years. Whereas he had eventually been forced to come to terms with his place inside the Sussex Police and in the world itself, one individual would never be forgiven for what that person had done to his career. At the stroke of one man's pen, Constable Alaister McMaster's whole career had suddenly come crashing down. From Regional Crime Squad to chasing taillights. It had been a bitter pill to swallow.

* * *

Alaister walked down the corridor and entered the private room. The man lying in the hospital bed was sleeping, connected by a series of tubes, wires and monitors. There was a comfortable hospital armchair in the corner of the room, the usual *hospital red*, if there was such a color, with a white hospital blanket draped over one arm. Alaister sat down in the armchair and waited patiently for a long time. Eventually the man in the bed sensed a presence in the room and opened an eye. When he realized who was sitting in the armchair across the small room from him, his eyes opened wide with first shock and then rage.

"What are you doing here, McMaster!" His voice was strained, the sound was more of a stifled cry, weak, almost inaudible.

"I heard you were dying, so I came to watch," replied Alaister coldly, never taking his eyes off the man in the bed.

Inspector Quinn tried to get up, his hands clawing at the sheets in fury. Because of the tube in his mouth and the tubes up his nose, his screams of rage were gargled. "Ffff … k you, McMaster!" were his last choking words on earth before he suddenly flopped back down on the bed. A series of alarm bells began ringing loudly in the room. Alaister could hear the muffled sounds of an alarm ringing down at the nurses' station.

He exited the room quickly, pausing only long enough to glance at the body lying on the hospital bed, now a grayish blue color, then calmly walked out of the room in the opposite direction to the nurses' station. As he ducked into another patient's room he could hear the sound of feet, nurses and doctors he suspected, dashing down the corridor to attend to their stricken patient.

"Sorry, mate, wrong room," Alaister said to the confused male sitting up in bed. He waited another minute before leaving the room and hurried down the staircase marked *Exit*. Once outside he walked briskly down the road to where he had concealed his police car behind an abandoned building. Like a man about to be caught in the bedroom with another man's wife, Alaister was out of his civilian clothes and back into his uniform within a matter of seconds. He drove quickly back to Storrington, hoping he had not been missed and drove around the outskirts of the village until it was time to go home. He was unaware that Communications had been trying to reach him for a call about cattle straying on the road.

The following morning Alaister sheepishly entered the Storrington Police Office, trying to be invisible.

"Where'd you get to yesterday evening, Alaister?" asked Sergeant Mike Harris. "Dispatch was calling you for ages."

"I went for a drive. I thought there was a problem with my radio, so I changed my batteries when I got back to the station."

"Car mobile dead too?"

"It was too; funny that. As soon as I pulled into the station, it started working again."

"I suppose you've heard the news?"

"What news would that be, Sergeant?"

"Inspector Quinn passed away yesterday evening in hospital. Had a massive heart attack. I don't suppose you'd know anything about that, Constable?"

"That's a strange thing to say, Sergeant, but I will say this. I wish I'd been there to see it. This is cause for a celebration, one down fifty to go."

"Remind me never to get on the wrong side of you, McMaster. I always said you had a screw loose. Oh, yes, before I forget, take down your mission statement from your locker before you retire."

"Which one, Sergeant?"

"You know the one. *For the past thirty years I have been led by bullies, bunglers and buffoons, I shall outlive them all.* Seems you've already started."

Alaister left the office without remorse. It was his *little secret*. The worst they could prove was a series of Police Act Charges. They'd not be able to prove theft of the police car, but would think of the criminal offence of taking and driving away and probably theft of the petrol he'd used. With a good lawyer it would all get washed under the carpet, especially as he was retiring anyway. But, to his knowledge, nobody even knew he had gone to pay his respects to the inspector.

"Life is good," he said as he walked around behind the office to his police car, parked in the garage at the rear.

* * *

Saturday morning Alaister McMaster and his wife, Jen, drove over to North Lancing to see their friends John Markham and his wife, Melissa.

"Morning, strangers," said John, his frame filling the doorway. "Hey, Melissa, guess who's here? Come on in. We were just talking about you and here you are."

His wife, Melissa, a petite woman with blonde hair walked out of the kitchen. She had been a very attractive woman before the attack, always very feminine, now she had her hair shaved short, wore no make-up and dressed more masculine. Her reconstructed face still bore the scars of the vicious assault. She smiled when she saw Alaister and Jen.

"Well, I know this sounds strange, John, but how would you like to come swimming with me this morning?" said Alaister, grinning broadly.

"What?" laughed John. "Are you nuts!"

"No, seriously. I don't want to talk about what I have to tell you other than in the middle of the swimming pool at the deep end. Trust me, it's important believe me. It's very important."

Alaister held his finger to his lips to indicate *someone* might be listening to their conversation. Slowly the penny began to drop.

"Has this got something to do with what happened to Melissa?" Alaister nodded.

"What's going on with you two?" Melissa asked.

"Male bonding, my love." John turned and grabbed his wife affectionately and went to kiss her on the cheek. She flinched and raised her arms instinctively as if to protect herself from an assault.

"Oh, God, I'm so sorry, my love."

"No, it's—it's all right." She took hold of him and drew his head down to hers and kissed him. "I'll go and find your trunks and get you a towel. There's coffee on, Jen, go help yourself, you know where everything is."

"Melissa and I will watch you two whales from the poolside, how about lunch out afterwards?"

"That would be lovely," replied Melissa, her voice carrying down from the airing cupboard upstairs.

Alaister sat at the kitchen table writing out a few brief sentences so that John and Melissa would have a better idea of what was going on. Alaister was paranoid that his own Police Service would now have him under surveillance, after all he had worked major crime cases before and that's exactly what he would have done. He didn't want to write too much, not knowing how close or how far they were from making a move against him. He told himself not to underestimate his opponent because he had no idea how much they knew already. He wrote:

No questions. I think they have surveillance on me. Will tell all at King Alfred swimming pool, Hove. Afterwards we go for pub lunch at Shepherd & Dog, Fulking. After I tell you what I know NEVER raise matter again!!! Say nothing to anybody! EVER!!!

John looked up from reading the note. "I think I know where this is going. If it's what I think it is, I feel joy and sadness at the same time, especially after what those two bastards did to my wife. Alaister, you're the only person in the world I'd let in my house that I trust about this. I won't insult you by asking if you're joking with me."

Melissa stood over the note, confused. Her husband's friend, her friend, Alaister, was behaving like some kind of secret agent. None of it made sense, especially when Alaister went over to the sink, took out a *Bic* lighter from his trouser pocket and set the note alight, washing the blackened remains down the sink. A black film stained the bottom of the sink around the plughole. Alaister scrubbed it away with a dishcloth as though it could still perhaps reveal something to his pursuers.

John had waited a long time for this moment. All that hurt deep inside him began to come out. He turned and hurried up to the bedroom where he buried his face in a pillow and cried, his deep sobs carrying downstairs.

Alone together one night in a patrol car, he confided in Alaister that he felt overwhelming guilt at not being there to protect his wife, and that he hadn't tracked her attackers down himself, torturing them every day for a week before killing them. He had played it out in his mind time and time again what he was going to do to them when he found them. And now, just like that, it was all over and he still couldn't do anything except cry into his pillow. Not only had they broken his wife, but they had broken him too. Melissa went upstairs after him, as she took hold of the banister rail Jen caressed her back, her own tears beginning to well up inside her.

Alaister and Jen sat patiently in the kitchen sipping their coffee and waited. Twenty minutes later their two best friends came back downstairs. No words were spoken.

Alaister whispered into his friend's ear. "John, we should take your car, mine's probably bugged. They're bound to have installed a tracking device as well." The two men looked at each other, John nodded and handed Alaister the keys.

"You drive, Alaister, I'm too upset, my nerves are shot."

"Okay, partner." Alaister slapped his friend on the shoulder and got in the driver's seat. John got in beside him, Melissa and Jen rode in the back.

No one spoke for a long time, fearful of what to say, just in case *they* had bugged John's car as well. When conversation resumed, though stilted, it centered around Alaister's retirement in August. He was going to have a beer down at the Whippletree in the village where he lived and policed and anyone who cared to say farewell to him, could join him there in the evening of his last day on the job.

Alaister suspected they were going to be tailed by probably three to four cars, maybe more, but unlikely. He went screaming around the Lancing Manor roundabout five times before accelerating south towards the seafront at over 100 mph. Without warning he would duck down one street, then re-emerge at another. He jumped the railway gates at Lancing Railway Station catching a glimpse in the rear view mirror of a frustrated surveillance driver unable to follow him through the closing gap. He smiled, even after all these years *he still had it.*

The drive along the seafront to the King Alfred swimming pool was slow going, traffic, as usual, was busy. They were lucky enough to pull into a parking space on Hove seafront, right in front of the public swimming pool, just as a car was pulling out of the spot. Jen and Melissa got themselves a coffee and sat on the terrace overlooking the swimming pool waiting for their husbands to enter the pool.

Alaister and John swam a couple of lengths before treading water in the middle of the deep end. The swimming pool was busy and noisy, as Alaister had hoped it would be.

"Well, out with it, Alaister, I didn't put this ill-fitting costume on just to attract the ladies."

Alaister looked about to make sure no one else was treading water or swimming near them before he spoke. He was also concerned about lip readers being employed and started to wonder about his own sanity as all these bizarre scenarios entered his mind. Between labored breaths he spoke to his friend.

"When we leave this pool, John, this matter is never to be mentioned again, never, ever. Do you understand?"

"Sure, of course. Hey, we've been partnered up through some hairy times, Alaister. You know I'm solid."

"I know that. How you tell Melissa is your own business, but you have to make sure she tells no one."

"She won't, trust me. Now come on, man, what is it?"

"McMahon and English are dead."

"What? You're joking. How?"

"How? I have my suspicions, but I'll never say, it would compromise my informant. All you need to know, John, is that justice has been done."

"How reliable is your informant?"

"As to, are they dead? One hundred percent reliable. As to how they died, that remains a mystery. My informant isn't saying and will never tell."

"Are you involved?"

"What kind of a question is that?"

"Sorry, it was kind of dumb."

"Anyway, I'm not, least not involved with their deaths, I just stumbled on the information. Believe me it's solid, I got it firsthand."

"You know who's responsible?"

"I think I do, but I can't say. If it ever came out it would lead straight to my informant."

"Do you know where their bodies are, I mean, have you seen them?"

"No, to both."

"You're sure this is reliable info. There's no way it could possibly be wrong? I mean I gotta be sure before I tell Melissa. You understand?"

"John, you know me better than that. Think about it. Why on earth would I be telling you all this, treading water in the middle of a public swimming pool if I didn't know it was true. And I know you're going to ask me, so I'll save you the trouble. The Brass knows that I know something. They know I got McMahon and English's fingerprints, but they don't know the truth about how I got them or where I got them. They suspect they're dead and think I've probably got something to do with it, that's why they've put surveillance on me. They're hoping I'll lead them to the so-called crime scene."

"Do you know where the crime scene is?"

"John, I know you want to know all the answers, you have a right to know, but I can't tell you that. Now stop asking so many questions, that way, if anything goes wrong, I'm the only one going down and probably my informant too."

"God, I'd like to shake his hand and buy him his own pub."

"Sometime in the next fifteen to twenty years I'll take you to where he'll be buried and you can pay your own respects to him then. It's no good giving me that quizzical look. No more questions, that's it. Let's do a few more lengths and go for lunch."

* * *

Detective Inspector Carter was at home when he decided to telephone his boss, Detective Chief Inspector Knight.

"Well?" said Knight abruptly.

"McMaster and his wife went to see the Markhams this morning."

"Interesting. Go on," said Knight slowly, deep in thought.

"They all went to the King Alfred in Hove. Only the two men went swimming."

"Ah, McMaster surveillance conscious already, unless your team screwed up."

"No, sir, that didn't happen. Unfortunately they went in Constable Markham's car, we had McMaster's vehicle bugged. Even McMaster's conversation with his wife on their way over to see the Markhams revealed nothing of interest, unless of course you're thinking of attending his leaving do at the Whippletree, sir," replied the detective inspector with genuine amusement.

"Are you trying to be funny, Carter!" shouted Knight down the phone. DI Carter had to take the phone away from his ear. He was smiling, enjoying this moment so much and Knight couldn't see how much difficulty he was having trying to stifle an outburst of laughter. "No, sir, not at all." He had to take the phone away again. His wife walked down the hallway with a puzzled look on her face. Carter drew an imaginary halo around his head with his finger to indicate to his wife that he was talking to *God*. She knew instantly whom he was referring to and smiled broadly. She disliked Knight almost as much as her husband did.

"Anything else of interest?"

"They went for lunch at the Shepherd and Dog in Fulking, sir."

"I know where it is, good choice though. What else?"

"That's about it, sir. They all drove back to the Markham's house, McMaster and his wife didn't go in, they got back in their own car and drove home."

"Did they say anything useful on their way home?"

"Mrs. McMaster asked her husband what they were going to do with their lottery winnings. She wasn't sure how they were going to invest the ten million they'd won."

"They're full of shit! Just trying to wind us up, which can only mean, if they haven't won the lottery they must suspect we're onto them."

"As you said yourself, sir, McMaster is surveillance conscious, so you're probably right about that."

"Anything else?" snapped the DCI.

"Nothing really, sir … Well, there is one thing of interest. It doesn't tell us anything if you're looking for words but, when they all left to go swimming, all four of them looked pretty stressed. When they returned, the Markhams looked as though they'd just won the bloody lottery. Mrs. Markham couldn't stop hugging McMaster and her husband kept shaking his hand and slapping him on the back. It was weird."

"Not really, Detective Inspector. When you've been around as long as I have and delved into the criminal mind as I have done, you get to understand these things. McMaster told Markham about what had happened to McMahon and English. In my opinion, he told them they were dead. Keep me informed. Oh, and double-check that thing about the lottery would you." Click went the phone just as DI Carter replied, "Yes, sir."

Knight didn't say goodbye to subordinates. He would have had a fit had he been able to see his detective inspector sticking two fingers up to the telephone repeatedly, and blowing raspberries at it, once he was sure he had properly replaced the receiver, as well as grabbing his bicep with the other hand and thrusting up his arm in the universal gesticulation of, *F' you!* He turned just in time to see his wife walking away down the hallway shaking her head.

"I don't think men ever grow up," she said as she walked into the kitchen. Her husband stood by the telephone table looking embarrassed and rather foolish.

* * *

For five months Detective Chief Inspector Knight kept the surveillance team on Constable Alaister McMaster. Even Alaister's own wife didn't know the real truth. Sometimes Alaister would walk into a store he knew well, walk out through the back door and run around to the front again, where he would stand on the street corner watching the store front. After a while he turned the tables on the surveillance team and began his own surveillance on them. He traded his new car in and bought a series of old bangers, changing them regularly. Finally, he went right up to a member of the surveillance team, a young female officer who had been tailing him along Montague Street in Worthing. The street was crowded with busy shoppers.

"Excuse me!" shouted Alaister at the top of his voice. "Can anyone tell me how to stop this young prostitute from propositioning me on the street. Lord save us!"

He then quickly walked away. She was kind of cute too and soon she had a number of males propositioning her. She was both embarrassed and furious, but dared not tell a soul what had happened for fear of being busted back to uniform patrol. After all, in her mind she thought she was something special, above that kind of drudgery.

At ten o'clock on Tuesday morning Detective Chief Inspector Hugh Knight's telephone rang on his desk.

"Good morning, Detective Chief Inspector, it's Madeline the chief's secretary. The chief would like to see you in his office in ten minutes."

"I'll be right up Madeline and how is Sir Richard this morning?" Knight wasn't inquiring about the chief's health, he wanted to know what kind of mood he was in.

"I'll tell him you're on your way then."
Madeline gave nothing away. She was very loyal
to her boss.

"Yes, right then, thank you, Madeline.
Goodbye." Knight wouldn't dare put the phone
down on Madeline. The thought of being sent to
Gatwick Airport in charge of parking did not
appeal to him.

Knight hated having to sit outside the
chief constable's office like a lowly constable,
waiting to be told by Madeline, *The chief
constable will see you now.*

Sir Richard Parker, the chief constable
for the Sussex Constabulary was on the
telephone in his office.

"Yes, Home Secretary, I'm about to give
him the news very shortly, in fact he's sitting
outside my office as we speak ... I agree one
hundred percent. It's not in the public's interest to
go raking up all this dirt and certainly not in the
interests of the Sussex Police ... Yes, very funny,
Home Secretary. Let sleeping dogs lie, very
good, very good. Right you are then. Consider it
done ... Not at all, Home Secretary, I'll see to it
personally ... Thank you, Home Secretary,
you're very kind ... Good bye to you, sir."

Sir Richard sat back in his chair smiling
up at the ceiling. He loved all that cloak and
dagger stuff.

"Sir Richard will see you now," said
Madeline as she put down her telephone.

"Thank you, Madeline. I keep forgetting, the knighthood."

Detective Chief Inspector Knight walked into the chief constable's office.

"Ah, Hugh, come on in. Thank you for coming so promptly, do sit down there's a good chap. Oh, before you sit down, hand me that tape recorder you've got in your pocket, there's a good fellow."

"I beg your pardon, Chief."

"Don't play innocent with me, Hugh, it's bloody common knowledge throughout the Service that you carry a bloody tape recorder man. Now hand the damn thing over!"

Feeling like a thief caught in the act, a very red faced Detective Chief Inspector Knight produced a small tape recorder from the inside pocket of his jacket.

"I, I—I wasn't taping our conversation, Chief Constable, I assure you," stammered the DCI.

"Well, it looks to me like the thing's recording, Hugh, I presume the red light being on might have something to do with it. Okay, let's keep it running for a bit of fun shall we?" Knight did not reply.

"This is the chief constable … Sit down man, sit down!" Knight reluctantly sat down opposite Sir Richard. "Yes, this is the chief constable of Sussex in company with Detective Chief Inspector Knight who has been caught with his pants down so to speak. On behalf of this police service, Detective Chief Inspector, I want to congratulate you for coming out of the closet today. I just got the news."

Knight looked shocked. This was news to him too. "Yes, Hugh, it's okay to be gay in the Sussex Police and you, Hugh, are going to lead our new initiative on the matter. You will be responsible for sensitivity training throughout the entire Service and you will be out their actively recruiting homosexuals and lesbians. I'm also putting you in charge of the Gay Pride Rally taking place on Brighton seafront in six weeks' time." It was all Sir Richard could do to keep a straight face.

Knight jumped to his feet. "Chief Constable, I really must protest in the strongest way!" Sir Richard roared with laughter, turned off the tape recorder and returned it to Knight after he had removed the cassette.

"This will go down a treat at the next Masonic dinner, Hugh," tears of laughter were now streaming down Sir Richard's cheeks. "Right. Enough of this frivolity, let's get down to business. Sit down man. You look as though you're about to collapse. Oh, the Gay Pride Rally, I wasn't joking about that. Make a good job of it there's a good fellow. You're not homophobic are you by any chance, Hugh?"

The detective chief inspector was very homophobic. "No, not in the least, sir," he replied lamely.

"Good, good, that's settled then." Without missing a beat, the chief constable roared, "Don't you ever bring a bloody tape recorder into any meeting I am attending without my prior consent. Do you understand, Detective Chief Inspector? Do that again and see how you enjoy foot patrol again on the streets of Brighton. Have I made myself clear enough!"

"Yes, sir, sorry, sir." Knight inwardly hated himself for being such a submissive coward. He wanted to pass wind, his nerves were so shot he daren't risk it.

"I'll get right to the point. I'll warn you now, I don't want a lot of questions or arguments. As of this moment, Operation Dark Shadow along with Operation Magnet is terminated. This comes right from the top, and I mean the top."

"But, Chief Constable, you can't be serious, we're beginning to make real progress. It won't be long before I have Constable McMaster's head on a platter and the rest of his body nailed to a wall!" Knight was almost screaming, but not quite, he knew better.

"Listen to me!" shouted Sir Richard forcibly. "I don't want Constable McMaster's head on anything other than his shoulders. In reality, Detective Chief Inspector, when it comes to being a coppers' cop, a bloody good street cop, you, Detective Chief Inspector, are not fit to carry Constable McMaster's briefcase!" Knight was about to protest. "Don't interrupt me. I am only going to tell you this once, Hugh. If you fail to comprehend please let me know, I do not want you leaving my office with any misunderstanding at all. This comes from a much higher position than I hold I assure you and, believe me, you don't want to mess with those people. Trust me on that one. So that you fully understand what's at stake here, for you that is, Hugh, let me remind you of something. Do you recall the scandal with the Labor politician dressed up as a drag queen in Piccadilly Circus?"

"Yes, sir, vaguely."

"That didn't happen by accident, man. He was becoming an embarrassment to the country, so someone from much higher than Sir Richard Parker had him drugged, doused with cheap whiskey, dressed up like a tart and left to be found by the media in Piccadilly Circus! Despite his protestations of innocence and a call for a public inquiry, nobody believed a word he had to say, even though he was telling the truth all along. His career was over, his wife left him and in the end he committed suicide. Well, let's put it this way, that was the official ruling on the matter. Gassed himself in his car in a remote area of Wales. And that's why we haven't heard a peep out of him since have we?"

"No, Chief, not to my knowledge."

"You will shut down Operation Dark Shadow forthwith. You will destroy every piece of paper connected with it. You will personally burn that five-pound note and you will personally crush that piece of bloody china into dust. If you do not do these things you will find yourself drunk, drugged up, wearing nothing but women's lingerie, lying on a bench in Piccadilly bloody Circus with a brass band around you playing Yankee Doodle Dandy. Do I make myself clear?"

"Yes, Chief, I'll see to it right away."

The chief constable lowered his voice and smiled paternally. "Thank you, Hugh, for your understanding in these matters. There are things that go on above us that we would do well not to ask questions about. Now, I will send my own team out to ensure you have carried out my wishes and if you have done so to my complete satisfaction I will be very grateful, Hugh, very grateful indeed. I'm sure you get my meaning. You have worked very hard on Operation Dark Shadow as well as Operation Magnet, excellent work on both counts I might add, and not to go unrewarded, Hugh, no certainly not. When you have done what I have asked you without complaint you are to telephone my secretary and tell her two things. She'll understand. Namely, that you have completed what was asked of you and secondly where you would like your next posting to be. I want this all done by five o'clock this afternoon. Any questions?"

"None, none at all, sir. That all seems perfectly straightforward. Thank you, Chief Constable, thank you very much."

"No, thank you, Hugh. That'll keep you busy for the rest of the day. Now off you go, there's a good chap."

When Knight closed the door behind him, Sir Richard muttered under his breath, *Thank heavens for arse kissers.* He then dialed Sir Oliver Compton-Smythe's number.

"Hello Oliver, Richard here, old boy ... Yes, fine thank you. Fancy a round of golf this afternoon? ... Say three o'clock? ... Right then, I'll meet you in the clubhouse ... You'll be pleased to know, I was just speaking to the Home Secretary regarding Constable McMaster and that as far as he's concerned justice has been done ... Funny, he said the same thing himself, *let sleeping dogs lie* ... Okay, see you at three and prepare for a thrashing." He walked out of his office in an upbeat mood, stopping to speak to Madeline.

At four o'clock that afternoon Madeline received the news from Detective Chief Inspector Knight that both Operation Dark Shadow and Operation Magnet had been disbanded and that he had attended to all the details asked for personally by the chief constable. His final words were, *Madeleine, should a vacancy become available, would you let the chief constable know that I would very much like to be put in overall charge of Administration.* She smiled and called Sir Richard on his cell phone with the news.

"Thank you, Madeline, I'm glad that's been attended to. I would have hated seeing Hugh in drag." She gave a knowing smile and prepared her desk for the next day's work.

Oliver Compton-Smythe was about to putt to stay one stroke ahead of the chief constable, he looked up when he heard what the chief constable was saying into his cell phone. The two men nodded at one another knowingly.

"Bugger!" shouted Oliver when his ball caught the lip of the hole, made a half circle and dribbled off down the green.

"Bad luck, old boy!" shouted Sir Richard, grinning from ear to ear. "It's anybody's game now."

Chapter Nine

It was August 10th. As of August 11th Constable Alaister McMaster would no longer be a police officer. His thirty-two years as a constable with the Sussex Police were finally over. He decided to pay a visit to Harry Davidson and remind his old friend that a taxi, courtesy of Paul had been arranged to take him to and from the Whippletree that evening for Alaister's farewell to the Sussex Police.

It was a sunny day, not too hot. Alaister had no intention of answering any radio calls. He decided to take out the old police issue Raleigh bicycle for the last time and take a long cycle ride, cycling north through the village of Storrington, before heading east, under the busy A24 via Ashington and eventually along Spithandle Lane. He was heading to Rose Cottage to have lunch with Harry. He told himself this would not be the last time he and Harry would share lunch and a beer together at Rose Cottage, but it would be the last time he did so wearing his police uniform as a member of the Sussex Police Constabulary.

Cycling along without a care in the world on one of the prettiest roads in England made Constable Alaister McMaster feel like this was one of the best days of his life. He even managed to cycle most of the laneway up to Rose Cottage. In the saddlebag he had a large bottle of vintage

Tullamore Dew Irish whiskey for Harry. He told himself he wouldn't drink too much today because he wanted to savor the cycle ride back along Spithandle Lane. *Ah, what the hell,* he finally said to himself. *I'll enjoy the ride all the more with a few good glasses of Irish whiskey in me.*

Harry was pleased to see him as were Jack and Jill. The two men shook hands firmly and prepared lunch together, like old times. During the summer months, on a nice day, they always made a point of sitting outside to eat. Today was no exception. They relaxed in a couple of old deckchairs, enjoying a huge beef sandwich stuffed with Harry's homegrown tomatoes, lettuce and radishes, sipping a glass of cold beer, with a *Tullamore Dew* whiskey chaser. The afternoon passed blissfully by, until reluctantly Alaister hauled himself out of the deckchair for the long ride back to the Storrington Police Office, for the last time.

"Thanks again, Alaister, for the whiskey. Don't worry, I'll be there tonight have no fear of that. Oh, before you go, take some of my homegrown vegetables with you. I've got quite the selection, the tomatoes have done really well this year, best year I've ever had. I'll give you some carrots and a nice lettuce too as well as some potatoes and green beans. They'll fit in that saddlebag of yours. Now you're sure you don't want a ride back into the village?"

"No, thanks, Harry. I'm going to enjoy my last cycle ride back to Storrington as a village bobby."

"Now mind you don't become a stranger, Alaister, I hope you'll still come to see me. Perhaps you and your wife could come up for a picnic, there are some lovely walks around these parts as you know."

"Harry, I'll never be a stranger. I always enjoy coming to see you and I know Jen would love to come and see you again. She always loves visiting you and Rose Cottage." Alaister stood up and brushed the crumbs from his tunic. "Right then, Harry, thanks again for lunch, I'll see you tonight then."

"That you will, Constable, that you will." The two men smiled, slapped each other's shoulders, knowing this was the last time Harry would be calling his friend *Constable*, though it would probably become a nickname he wouldn't be able to shake free of.

Constable Alaister McMaster threw his leg over the huge leather saddle of the old Raleigh bicycle for the last time and began to cycle away down the lane, homegrown produce sticking out from under the large black leather saddlebag.

"You enjoy those vegetables, Constable McMaster!" shouted Harry after him. "They've got plenty of body in them!"

It wasn't until Alaister turned onto Spithandle Lane and cycled a few hundred yards along the road that the realization of what Harry Davidson had just said to him struck him like an explosion of light inside his head. The front wheel of the bicycle struck a rut as he wobbled too close to the grass verge, the bicycle went down, Alaister thrust out his hands and rolled into the verge, unhurt, but very embarrassed. Fortunately, there were no other people on the road and no car drivers or passengers to witness his faux pas. Had they seen him, he would have looked quite comical, legs wide apart, feet off the pedals, his police helmet at a rakish angle on his head and then head-over-heels over the handlebars into the long grass growing along the side of the road.

Alaister sat smiling next to his bicycle and then broke out laughing. He brushed himself off as best he could, but even to a casual observer, the grass stains and dust on his uniform were clear evidence that he had taken a tumble from his bicycle, but he didn't care, it would be just another story circulating throughout the village. *Looks like Constable McMaster got drunk on his last day on the job and fell off his bike.*

Alaister lifted the bicycle back onto its wheels, pulling out tufts of grass and weeds from the spokes and rearranging the leather saddle bag. Sticking out from under the corner of the saddle bag were two medium-size carrots, their green fern-like leaves still attached. Alaister wheeled the bicycle over to a large oak tree, its huge canopy casting a cool shadow across the road. He lent the old bicycle against the tree, pulled off his tie, opened his shirt collar and undid his tunic. He stood for a while listening to the rural sounds around him before carefully pulling out the two carrots, wiping the dirt from them with his hands. Symbolically, Alaister raised the two carrots up to the sky, squeezing them tightly together in his left hand.

As if giving a speech to the whole village he shouted, "May you bastards both rot in hell!" He then bit off the two ends of the carrots and began to chew them, surprised at how sweet they tasted. When he had eaten the carrots he cast away their tops into the field nearby. "Revenge is so sweet," he called out again. He was suddenly flooded with thirty-two years of pent-up emotions. He left a smear of dirt from Harry's vegetable garden across his face as he wiped away tears of frustration, bitterness, sadness and joy.

"God bless you, Harry Davidson," the words came out choked, he was hurting so much inside. Like so many other veteran police officers before him, he too carried the pain of everyone else's suffering throughout his long policing career, hidden deep in the dark recesses of his soul.

He cried for the children sexually abused by those they had trusted; the ultimate betrayal. They had been hard cases to work on. Each time he had interviewed an abused child, a piece of him died inside his soul. He cried for the old people whose homes had been violated, their precious belongings stolen in a burglary, often they passed away not long afterwards, broken themselves. He cried for the good people, young and old slaughtered on the roads by drunk drivers. Now he wouldn't have to pick-up their body parts anymore or find himself standing in their brain matter. He cried for all the innocent murder victims, whose crime scenes he had watched over for days on end. Finally, he swore aloud at all the lousy supervisors he had been forced to endure throughout his career. He gave the thumbs up to the precious few who had been true leaders and wished there could have been more like them in the Service. He felt so alone, shocked by what had just happened to him. He had thought about this day for so long and now it was here. The joy and euphoria he was expecting to feel hadn't come to him, perhaps it never would. Policing had been his life. The silence was broken by his radio. *November Two Zero Nine, please attend the Storrington Police Office.*

Constable Alaister McMaster composed himself, took a few deep breaths before cycling back down Spithandle Lane for the long cycle ride into Storrington for the very last time. He knew his sergeant and colleagues and their wives were waiting there for him, for their own private farewell. There to watch him hang up his hat for the last time. Erin would be there along with John and Melissa Markham. His wife, Jen, would be there too. How he loved that woman, she had stood beside him through thick and thin. A year from now she would be retiring too and they could start their lives all over again. They could start travelling like they'd talked about so often. These were the thoughts that began to fill Constable Alaister McMaster's mind as he cycled blissfully along Spithandle Lane, his tunic flapping insolently in the breeze.

The shadows were getting longer as the afternoon progressed towards early evening. Rooks were making their usual raucous noise as they prepared to roost in the tall beech trees for the night. It was going to be a wonderful cycle ride back to the police office and Alaister wasn't in any hurry, he was going to enjoy his last ride on his old police bicycle. The smell of the grasses, the wild flowers and the smell of the fields filled his nostrils, smells he never tired of.

"Harry Davidson, you crafty old bugger."

End

Ron Ady Crouch books also published by Books We Love available at Amazon.com

O'Malley's Cottage

Coming in 2014
Lettuce Beware

About The Author

Ron was born in Brighton, England and has worked in the U.K. and Canada for over thirty years as a police officer. He has extensive international travel experience while working with the British Merchant Navy as a navigator, where he travelled extensively in the Middle East and throughout Europe. He is an avid outdoorsman, enjoying wilderness camping throughout the year. With a love of nature, he also paints with watercolors.

Ron has always had a passion for writing which started in his early years. He enjoys writing in various genres, both adult and children's fiction. He continues to write from his home in Ontario, Canada

Books We Love Ltd.
http://bookswelove.net